"Jabberwocky!" Corey screamed. She moved to go after him, but Topher held her back.

"It's too late," he said, his voice flat.

"*No—no—no!*" Corey tried to run. Topher shook her, his hands gripping, hurting her arms.

"Stop it!" he yelled. "We've got to get out of here. If we don't, we'll die!"

COREY'S FIRE

Lee Wardlaw

cover illustration by Steve Brennan

People do not lack strength, they lack will.
—Victor Hugo

For Mom, Scott, and John:
Who still get shivers when the
Santa Anas blow . . .

Published by Willowisp Press,
a division of PAGES, Inc.
801 94th Avenue North, St. Petersburg, Florida 33702

PRINTING HISTORY
Avon Flare edition 1990

Printed in the United States of America

2 4 6 8 10 9 7 5 3 1

ISBN 0-87406-784-7

CHAPTER
1

COREY AWOKE FRIDAY MORNING with a jolt. Had she really heard a motorcycle revving at the foot of her bed? She sat up quickly, brushing dreams and auburn hair from her eyes. Her heart pounded furiously, but the room was quiet. Only her cat, Jabberwocky, lay curled at her feet, purr-snoring lightly.

"Okay, Jab," she said with a yawn. "Was that you making all that noise?"

The cat rumbled louder and Corey laughed. "Yeah, I'll bet," she said.

Resting her head on one hand, she idly scratched behind Jabberwocky's black silken ears. "Wild dreams," she murmured, and closed her eyes. Soon the frantic thud-thudding of her heart slowed. Corey dimly realized she was slipping back toward sleep.

Suddenly, the roar of an engine filled the room. Corey jumped, wincing as Jabberwocky's claws dug through the sheet into her foot.

"I didn't dream it," she grumbled. *"Him* again. Him and his stupid motorcycle."

She yanked the sheet over her head, wrinkling her nose at the bitter smell of exhaust that drifted through the open window. "Yuck!"

Jabberwocky sneezed in agreement.

Why, oh, why, hadn't someone *nice* moved in next door? Corey thought. Sure, he was gorgeous all right, but nice? Huh! She punched the roof of her bed-cave. Nice and hostile, maybe.

A hot flush of anger prickled Corey's face. It had been two months since her first—and last—meeting with Christopher West, yet the incident remained painfully fresh in her mind.

"Why not invite him to Ericka's swimming party?" her mother suggested that day in August. "The real estate agent told me Topher—that's his nickname—and his mother just moved here from Los Angeles. They don't know a soul in town. Topher's sixteen, a couple years older than you, but I'm sure he'd appreciate meeting your friends."

Corey's stomach twitched uncomfortably. "But, Mom, I've never even met the guy. I mean, what if he's an ax murderer or a Hell's Angel or something? Have you seen that motorcycle of his?"

Mrs. Johnson laughed softly. "Honey, I met Topher, and believe me, he doesn't wear chains or tattoos. He actually seemed a little shy, just like you. I'm sure it'll be easier for him to start school knowing a few people."

"Not if he's like me," Corey argued. "I know lots of kids from junior high, but every time I think about starting high school, my stomach goes into labor. Harder teachers, new classes, finding my way around—" She winced. "The only thing that keeps me from giving birth to a bouncing baby ulcer is Ericka."

Ericka had been Corey's best friend since kindergarten. The two of them did everything together. Junior high drill team, mall cruising on Saturday afternoons, baby-sitting, boy-watching, and two-hour phone conversations, every night. Ericka *loved* to talk.

"Hey, maybe I could get Ericka to call him," Corey said with a grin. "She could make conversation with a soap dish."

"You can't expect Ericka to do everything for you." Mrs. Johnson's voice held a note of impatience. "After all, Topher's your neighbor, not hers."

Silence.

"Go on," her mother urged gently. "Ask Topher to the party. The worst he can do is say no."

Her mother had been wrong.

Topher had *laughed* at her—a short, disdainful laugh as cold as his ice-blue eyes.

"Don't do me any favors, kid," he said. "I don't need you. Or your little friends."

Kid. Little friends.

Corey froze with shock, tears of humiliation and anger pricking her eyes. She longed to tell

7

him, in a cool, calm tone, that he was tactless. Rude. Insensitive. Insulting. In other words, a jerk. But what good would it do? He'd only zap her again, maybe worse this time. And it would take her ten days to think up a worthy comeback.

Without a word, Corey turned away. She vowed never to speak to him again, never to give him another chance to make her feel so foolish. So far she had kept that promise, though Topher was hard to avoid.

Every time she passed his house, she saw him working in the driveway, his dusty blond curls bent over an array of greasy tools and motorcycle parts. And if her first day of school hadn't been bad enough, she discovered that Topher shared her algebra class.

Probably why I hate algebra, Corey thought.

Outside, the engine growled again. With a frustrated gesture, Corey swept back the sheet.

Why did things always have to change? Two months ago, her life was perfect, secure. Now everything had turned upside-down. A motorcycle maniac lived next door, her brother Pete had left home for college, and just about all her friends had started dating. All except Ericka.

"If this keeps up, I'll have to enter our names in the *Guinness Book of World Records*," Ericka joked gloomily last week. " 'Girls Have First Date at Age Seventy-five.' Hey, maybe we'll win a wheelchair or something!"

The phone rang, scattering Corey's thoughts. She lunged for the bedside receiver, catching it before the second ring. Ericka. Had to be. No one else would dare call so early.

"Joe's Bar and Grill," Corey said, suppressing a giggle.

A long pause. *Oh, no,* she thought, stricken. It was one of her dad's patients . . .

Then a male voice said: "A burger and fries, please. To go."

"Pete!" Corey gave a cry of relief and delight at the sound of her brother's voice. With the exception of one funny postcard, she hadn't heard from him in six weeks. "Pete, how *are* you? I thought you were Ericka."

"A lot of people make that mistake. We both have the same sexy ring."

Corey grinned. She pictured her brother sprawled lazily, much like Jabberwocky, his freckled face beaming.

"Hey, did I wake you?" he asked.

"Are you kidding? I've been awake for ages." She shot a glance at the window. "Thanks to Topher's thirty-five-horsepower alarm clock."

She meant it as a joke, but an edge of bitterness had crept into her voice. If Pete noticed, he didn't mention it. He continued in his slow drawl. "So, the King of Motocross is at it again, huh? Well, just leave him to me, Sis. What'll it be? Peanut butter in his gas tank? Tarantulas in his helmet? I know, I'll pump his tires full of helium. Up, up, and away!"

Corey laughed. Just like Pete, she thought. Pronouncing marvelous tortures of devious revenge, all in that teasing, laid-back tone of his. Yet she caught a hint of sincerity in his words.

"Listen, Corey," Pete was saying. "Tell Mom and Dad I'm coming home for the weekend. I don't have any classes on Fridays this semester, so I'll be there by late afternoon. You gonna be home tonight?"

"Oh, rats, Pete. No. Mom and Dad are going to a Dental Society party, and I'm spending the night at Ericka's. We're planning her Halloween party."

"Ah, yes," Pete said, "the annual extravaganza. Okay, no sweat. We'll go out for a fancy family dinner tomorrow. My treat. Let's see, do you prefer Taco Bell or McDonald's?" His voice grew serious. "Hang in there, Sis. Don't let Topher, or anything else, get you down. You're gonna be A-OK."

Before Corey could reply, Pete said, "Gotta go. Catch ya later."

Corey replaced the receiver, smiling to herself. Nothing got by Pete. Although he'd always played the role of big brother, protecting her from teasing bullies or barking dogs, in the last few months he seemed particularly aware of her low moods. More than once during the summer, he had canceled plans with his buddies to spend more time with her, taking her for day hikes in their foothill neighborhood or just listening patiently when she talked of her nervousness about high school. He had even started to defend her position during family discussions, and together they had successfully negotiated a summer trip to Hawaii, instead of their usual vacation to the lake.

Corey's heart squeezed with happiness. How great it would be to have her brother home again! Her parents would be pleased, too. They hadn't expected to see Pete until Thanksgiving.

"Come on, Jabber. Wake up." Corey tugged playfully at the cat's tail, then opened her closet. She tapped a fingernail against her teeth as she searched for something cool to wear.

Though Halloween was only two weeks away, Corey still found it hard to believe summer was gone. Autumn had arrived in Southern California without the usual chilly mornings and drizzle of coastal fog. Instead, hot desert Santa Anas blew over the mountains. They had caused temperatures in Santa Barbara to soar near one hundred the last few days.

Corey didn't mind the heat. She loved the Santa Anas. Besides bringing perfect beach weather, they stirred a tingle of excitement inside her, evoking the same hurry-up-and-get-here feeling she experienced the day before her birthday or Christmas.

In honor of Pete's homecoming, Corey finally chose her favorite sundress. It had tiny green flowers that turned her eyes a wild-mint shade. As she dressed, a warm breath of Santa Ana blew into the room, tickling her cheek. Again

11

she felt that familiar zing of anticipation.

A sudden crash startled her. Corey whirled. Her dainty bedside lamp lay in crystal splinters on the floor. The curtain behind it billowed in a frenzied dance of wind.

"Oh, no," Corey said softly. She moved to sweep up the pieces, sadness filling her. She'd had that lamp since her fifth birthday: a special gift from her grandmother. Now it was gone.

And so was the special feeling of excitement. A heavy, ominous feeling replaced it, like a cloud suddenly covering the sun. For a moment, Corey thought that something awful waited to happen to her. She shivered despite the heat. Then the strange feeling disappeared.

Static electricity? Or maybe losing her treasured lamp had caused the eerie feeling. Well, she'd just have to take Pete's advice and not let it get her down. Not the lamp, not the feeling, no, not even Topher. Today was Friday. Hot, beautiful Friday. Pete was coming home, and tonight she'd help Ericka plan the best Halloween party yet.

Gently, Corey placed the remains of her lamp in the trash basket. Then she shut her window with a determined bang. Yes, today was the beginning of a great weekend. What could possibly go wrong?

CHAPTER
2

A FEW MINUTES LATER, Corey hurried downstairs to the kitchen, Jabberwocky at her heels. She found her mother, dressed in jogging shorts and T-shirt, slicing cantaloupe for breakfast.

"Morning, luv," Jan Johnson said with a smile. "Was that Ericka on the phone?"

"Uh-uh. Pete. And guess what? He's coming home today!"

"Anything wrong?"

"Naw," Corey said. "His roommate kicked him out. Got tired of Pete keeping his car in their dorm room."

Mrs. Johnson laughed appreciatively. "Honestly, Corey, you're terrible. Try not to give Pete such a bad time about that car, hmmm? He worked hard to earn the money for it, you know. Just wait till there's something you want bad enough to work for. Then you'll understand how much that car means to Pete."

"I already understand," Corey said. "He only washes it about eight times a day. But don't worry. I'll be nice."

Corey scooped Jabberwocky into her arms, stroking him as she watched her mother arrange the cantaloupe slices on a large plate. She liked watching her mother. It gave her a safe, secure feeling seeing the efficient yet cheerful way her mother handled even the simplest things in their lives.

Mom's good at everything, Corey thought. Everything from cooking to jogging to bookkeeping for Dad's dental practice. But especially photography.

Corey glanced into the dining room and felt a swell of pride. Every wall in their house held breathtaking seascapes and mountain views, frozen in a split-click of her mother's camera. Mrs. Johnson had become so skilled that Corey's father had converted the downstairs bathroom into a permanent darkroom. A few of her mother's photographs were currently on display in a friend's gallery downtown.

Corey sighed. Perhaps one day she'd make a miraculous discovery: that she'd inherited more from her mother than straight auburn hair.

"Better feed Jab," Mrs. Johnson said. "Dad'll be down for breakfast soon."

"Okay." Corey placed her cat on the floor, then opened a can of cat food. "Mmmm, you'll like this, Jabber," she said, spooning a portion

14

into Jabberwocky's dish. "Smells like dead sea gulls."

Mrs. Johnson grimaced. "Corey, not before breakfast."

"Sorry." Corey picked up the silverware her mother placed on the tiled counter. "Okay if I set the picnic table? Might be cooler outside."

"Sure," her mother said. "Take the juice out, too, please."

Corey stepped outside and arranged place settings for three, then leaned against the deck railing, chin propped on her hands. A gust of Santa Ana flirted with her hair. She brushed back a strand thoughtfully.

Such a breathtaking view. In the fourteen years she'd lived here, she'd never grown tired of it. Sycamore Canyon had to be the most beautiful place in the world.

The Johnsons lived in a rambling, redwood house that overlooked the foothill neighborhood. Corey watched as eucalyptus trees bent lazily in the wind, hiding, then revealing, other homes nestled against the chaparral-covered hills. She thought the canyon looked like a great golden sea, gently rolling, unfolding, down to the city. If she stood on tiptoe, she could see the real ocean, shimmering in a blue line across the tops of the trees.

She could never leave this place. Couldn't imagine finding another home so beautiful, so peaceful, so—

A motorcycle roared by, destroying the early

15

morning quiet. Corey banged her fist on the railing. Topher again.

"Such hideous colors," her mother murmured behind her. She placed the plate of cantaloupe on the table. "Pete says a lot of dirt bikes are bright like that for racing. But yellow and black—not my favorite."

"It looks like a giant bee," Corey observed. And he stings, too, she thought. "I wish you and Dad would do something about him, Mom. Topher rides that bike through everybody's property, tearing up all the trails. And it's so darn noisy." She gestured sharply. "I wish he'd never moved here."

"There's not much we can do about that," Mrs. Johnson replied. "But maybe Dad could talk to Mrs. West. Make sure Topher only rides on his own property." She gazed out over the canyon, frowning slightly. "Must admit, though, I've been concerned about that cycle. Everything's so dry this fall. Especially with the Santa Anas. We need rain. I'm afraid one spark from Topher's cycle could start the whole neighborhood on fire."

The edge of apprehension she heard in her mother's voice gave Corey a hollow feeling inside. She tried to laugh it off. "Hey, Mom, what's wrong with you this morning? Shoot a roll of film and forget to take off the lens cap?"

Mrs. Johnson sighed, then gave Corey a reassuring squeeze. "Oh, don't mind me. Guess I'm just feeling a little low. It's this heat." She

16

laughed. "I have my sunny reputation to consider, so please don't tell your dad."

"I won't." Corey returned her mother's hug. "Don't tell me what?"

Corey turned to find her father standing behind her.

Mrs. Johnson shot Corey a look. "Uh, that we're only having cereal and fruit this morning. Too hot for anything else."

Corey sat across from her parents at the picnic table, and dug into a bowl of shredded wheat.

"Hey," her father said. "No good-morning grin for your favorite orthodontist? Now that your braces are off, you've got to advertise that beautiful smile. Good for my business."

Corey's spoon dripped milk as she held it in midair. She bared her straight, white teeth at him comically.

"That's better," he teased. "Jan, just look at my handiwork."

His wife rolled her eyes. "I've seen it, dear." She winked at her daughter.

Corey winked in return, smiling to herself. The gentle teasing was a morning ritual she loved. How strange it must be to have parents you couldn't tease, couldn't talk to. So many kids never stopped complaining about their parents. Imposing unfair restrictions. Never listening. Not understanding. Corey shook her head slightly to dispel the thought. She felt fortunate to have a mom and dad she not only loved, but liked as well.

"Corey, look at that," Dr. Johnson said. "I think Jabber's cornered a mouse."

Corey turned. "Where?"

"Not in the house, I hope," Mrs. Johnson said mildly.

"No, over there." Dr. Johnson pointed to the field that separated their home from Topher's. Jabberwocky's sleek body crouched low in the dry weeds. He seemed to be peering into a hole.

"Well, what do you know," Mrs. Johnson said. "I thought that cat was well past his mouse-catching prime."

"He might be a little deaf," Corey replied, "but he's still a pretty good mouser." She put a finger to her lips. "Now, please. You'll break his concentration."

She sat watching the cat so intently, it took her a moment to notice the familiar sound of an approaching motorcycle.

Topher again, she thought in disgust. Out of the corner of her eye she saw him riding down the road behind her house. Then her mouth opened in horror.

At full speed, Topher pulled off the road and into the field. He headed straight for Jabberwocky.

Corey leaped up, knocking the picnic bench over with a crash. She barely noticed it. Inside her, a scream struggled to get out—to stop Topher, to warn Jabberwocky. Too late. The large knobby wheels of the cycle spun toward the cat in a spray of dust.

"He'll be killed!" she cried. But at the last second, Jabberwocky lifted his head and leaped aside.

Corey gave a strangled moan. She saw that Topher still had no intention of riding home. Instead, he turned and chased Jabberwocky, his cycle bumping and growling as he zigzagged through the fields. Clouds of dust boiled up behind the bike, shrouding Topher in an eerie brown fog.

He looks like the Headless Horseman, Corey thought. Topher's hair and face were almost completely hidden by his black helmet, and his T-shirt flapped behind him like a cape. Perched atop the garish yellow bike, he rode like a wild, faceless phantom.

For a moment, Corey lost sight of her cat. Then, in a streak of black fur, Jabberwocky flew past her across the deck and into the house.

Corey ran after him. She saw his tail, half hidden beneath the living room couch. On hands and knees, she peered into his hiding place.

"Come out, Jabber," she coaxed softly. "It's okay now."

Mrs. Johnson stood behind her. "Is he all right?"

"Yes. No. Oh, I don't know." Corey looked up at her mother, tears filling her eyes. "He's probably having a heart attack. He's too old to be chased like that."

"I'm sure he's more scared than hurt," Mrs. Johnson said, her tone soothing. "Let's get him out from under there and take a look."

Gently, Corey and her mother tugged at the cat until he crawled from beneath the couch. Corey inspected him closely.

"His heart's flying, but he's okay," she said. She held him close, stroking his dusty fur.

Now, certain that Jabberwocky was safe, anger replaced Corey's panic and concern.

"How could Topher *do* that, Mom?" Her voice sounded high and strained. "He's the most incredible jerk I've ever met. I've had enough of him and his motorcycle. You've got to do something about him."

"I know, sweetheart," her mother said. "Don't worry. Dad's gone next door to speak with Mrs. West. He'll make sure this doesn't happen again."

"I think you should call the police. Have Topher arrested."

Mrs. Johnson smoothed Corey's hair. "Let's keep this neighborly, okay? Dad will take care of everything. I promise. Has he ever let you down?"

Corey shook her head.

"Well, then. Oh-oh. Almost eight o'clock. Better get going or you'll miss your bus."

"But Jabber—"

"He'll be fine," Mrs. Johnson assured her. "You know I'll watch him."

Corey nodded and surrendered the cat to her mother. Then she gathered up her books and raced outside. The school bus idled noisily at the end of the driveway. She ran toward it.

Topher—is—a—jerk! she thought, her stomach clenching with every word. How she'd love to be in her father's place right now. She'd tell Mrs. West exactly how rotten her son was. And this time, she'd lay into Topher, too. He could insult her. He could destroy the canyon with that stupid motorcycle. But he wouldn't, *wouldn't* get away with this.

Corey reached the bus before it pulled away and flung herself into the nearest seat. Several kids looked up at her in surprise.

As the bus jostled along the canyon road, she relaxed a little, trying to recapture her earlier feeling of excitement. Ericka would get on at the next stop. They could talk about the Halloween party and their plans for tonight and . . .

Corey sighed. It was no use. She'd lost the exciting tingle for good. All that remained was her clenched stomach and the nagging, ominous feeling that the day would only get worse.

CHAPTER 3

"COREY, WHAT'S WRONG?" Ericka sat quickly beside her friend, her voice hushed and concerned. "What happened? And don't say 'Nothing.' I can tell." She studied Corey's face critically for a moment. "The corners of your mouth are all pinched, the way they were that day in the gym when Susan Rehler borrowed your new sweatshirt without asking. And you're tense. Very tense. Your arms are crossed, your legs are crossed—I'll bet even your *teeth* are crossed!"

"Maybe I'm just cold," Corey said with a laugh.

"Are you kidding? When it's already ninety degrees? *Please.* Hey, we've known each other so long that sometimes I think I know you're upset before you do. Now come on, what's the matter?"

"Loan me a wrench," Corey said with a grim smile. "A big one. I want to take Topher's cycle apart, piece by piece." Briefly, she explained the events of the morning.

"Oh, poor Jabber!" Ericka touched Corey's arm. "No wonder you're so mad. Topher's been a real pain since Day One. I wonder what his problem is?"

As Ericka leaned back in the seat, Corey caught a whiff of coconut-scented perfume. She'd brought Ericka a bottle as a souvenir from Hawaii. Her friend loved the stuff so much, she wore it every day.

One whiff of Ericka and *wow!*—instant time machine back to summer. The light fragrance, combined with that long, white-blond hair and the even, toasty color of her skin, accented Ericka's California image.

She could get a tan from a light bulb, Corey thought with a twinge of envy.

"Topher is so weird," Ericka said suddenly. "But you know? He's got the most interesting face."

"Oh-oh!" Corey held up her hands in mock alarm. "Here comes the great psychoanalysis."

"No, listen a minute, Corey. I've watched Topher at school. He always eats alone, doesn't talk to anybody, doesn't have any friends. But he doesn't seem to care. He's different from anyone I've ever known. Yet in some ways, he reminds me of you."

"Oh, *thanks!*"

"Wait. You can tell he really feels things. He's emotional like you are, you know? Only you release your feelings, by crying. Topher's face looks sort of tight. Like things are building up inside, and one day he'll just explode."

"Oh, great," Corey said. "I've got Mount St. Helens living right next door."

Ericka continued in a contemplative tone. "I'll bet he had a terrible childhood. Maybe his pet hamster died and his dad flushed it down the toilet." A tiny squeal. "*Eeeek*—Topher, I'm dwownding!"

Corey fell against the window, laughing. "Gross, Ericka. You've been reading too many psych books. But I *do* feel better."

"Just call me Dr. Joyce Brothers," Ericka said cheerfully. "You'll get my bill at the end of the month. Now, down to business. Halloween's only two weeks away, and I still don't know what to wear at my own party."

"Oh! Almost forgot. I came up with a costume idea for both of us." Corey dug through her purse for a pen. "Let me work out a few details first."

Hunched over her notebook, she sketched furiously. She glanced up only once when a motorcycle sped past the bus, stirring vivid images of Jabberwocky running, Jabberwocky trembling. Corey's heart gave a little squeeze.

"Come on, slowpoke," Ericka begged. "Let me see the sketch."

Corey covered the notebook with her hand. "No, don't look. I'll show you at lunch."

"Lunch! That's four periods away!"

"It'll go fast," Corey promised.

But the morning dragged endlessly. The

classrooms were hot and stuffy, the teachers irritable. By fourth period, Corey felt limp with the heat. She peeked at her watch. Fifteen more minutes until lunch. It seemed an eternity.

She sketched a surfboard in the margin of her American lit notes. Oh, those cold waves would feel so good right now. But she wasn't brave enough to skip school. At least not without getting a double dose of the guilts. Her parents had seen to that.

She glanced at her watch again and sighed. So, here she sat. Her and her heatstroke. She could picture tonight's headlines: GIRL DIES IN HOT CLASSROOM. PROPER UPBRINGING BLAMED.

At last the noon bell rang. Quickly, Corey escaped the main building, grateful to be outside, even under the fierce sun. As she hurried to meet Ericka, a gust of wind ballooned the skirt of her sundress up around her waist. Several guys standing nearby whistled and clapped.

"Stupid wind," Corey muttered, flushing. The Santa Anas lost some of their appeal.

Moments later, she found Ericka waiting for her in their usual lunch spot. Both girls sank down into the dry grass.

"It's—so—hot," Corey said breathlessly. "Thank God that class is over."

Ericka twisted her long hair into a knot at the base of her neck. "I thought lit was a fun class."

"Usually. Yesterday, Miss Winkler wore a walrus mustache and imitated Mark Twain. Today she just lectured—and sweat."

Ericka giggled. "Okay, where are those sketches? I'm dying to see."

Corey tossed her friend the notebook. "It's the King and Queen of Hearts," she explained. "Like in *Alice in Wonderland*. See, we can wear red leotards and tights, and make a couple of crowns. We'll use large pieces of poster board for the card part. You're a good artist, so maybe you can copy the King and Queen faces off some real playing cards."

"Sure, that'd be easy," Ericka said. "How do we wear the cards?"

"Just hook them together with straps, here—" She pointed at the sketch. "—and here, then slip the straps over our shoulders."

"Corey, you're a genius. I love it." Ericka closed the notebook and lay back with a sigh. "When you come over tonight we can—" She stopped.

"What's the matter?" Corey asked. Ericka had sat up again, squinting into the sun.

"Isn't that Topher? He's coming this way."

"Gimme a break, Ericka. Not funny." Corey turned—and felt a sudden chill. It *was* Topher. This morning she had wanted nothing more than to tell him off, face to face. Now as he approached, her chest filled with apprehension.

"He looks ready to kill," Ericka whispered. "What did your dad say to him this morning?"

"I don't know." Corey's voice sounded hollow. Ericka was right. Topher's face looked tight. Ready to explode.

He stood in front of her now, blocking out the sun. His dark clothes and motocross boots made him seem taller than usual.

"I want to talk to you," he demanded. He glanced at Ericka with cold eyes. "Alone."

"I—I'm eating right now," Corey stammered. She took a bite of apple and held it up as if to verify her words.

Topher stared at her for a long minute. He shrugged. "Have it your way. I'm only here at the persuasive request of your father. When do you think you can fit me into your—" he paused, "—terribly busy schedule?"

Corey swallowed hard, almost choking on the bit of apple.

"Well?" Topher asked.

"Well," Corey said lamely. "I guess we can talk sometime tonight."

"Fine. Seven-thirty. Your house." He shoved his hands into the pockets of his jeans and strode away. Mutely, Corey watched him go.

"She'll be waiting in breathless anticipation," Ericka said.

Corey winced. "Ericka! He could've heard you."

"I don't care. Who does he think he is, anyway? Hey, but you were great, Corey. You really held your ground."

"Thanks." Actually, she hadn't done anything, except sit there with her face turning red.

"I wonder what he wants to talk to you about?"

"It doesn't matter," Corey said with a sudden fierceness. "He's not going to do any of the talking. I am. He's made me feel stupid and helpless for the last time. Tonight—" She took a deep breath. "Tonight I'm going to tell him everything that's been on my mind."

"Good for you!" Ericka squeezed Corey's arm in reassurance. "But please don't tell him *everything*. You won't make it to my house till tomorrow morning!"

Corey forced a smile. "Okay, I'll just hit the highlights. That's gonna be hard enough."

"You'll be okay," Ericka said confidently.

Corey sighed. "I wish I could be as sure." She wiped a trickle of sweat from her forehead. "Let's get out of this sun. Between the heat and the elephant hopping around in my stomach, I'll probably throw up in algebra."

Algebra! She'd completely forgotten. The elephant did a triple spin, then belly flopped into her lunch.

"Oh, no," she moaned.

"What's wrong?"

"Ericka, Topher's in my algebra class. He'll probably shoot me dirty looks all period with those ice-cold eyes!"

"So don't look at him," Ericka said firmly. Corey pressed her hands against her stomach. It was going to be a terrible afternoon.

CHAPTER
4

AT LAST. THREE O'CLOCK.

Corey climbed aboard the school bus, plopping her books on the seat beside Ericka in a gesture of finality.

"So how'd it go?" Ericka asked.

"Fine," Corey said. "After worrying all afternoon, I got saved by the bell. Literally." She brushed back a strand of damp hair that clung annoyingly to her face. "Right after class started, we had that fire drill. Topher never came back to class. He just disappeared. Mr. Yenke was furious."

"Wow," Ericka breathed. "Wish I'd been as lucky when I had Yenke this morning. I hate him." Her voice lowered to a growl. "You vill learn thees algebra and you vill like eet—or else!"

Corey laughed at Ericka's impersonation. She, too, found Mr. Yenke's German accent as unintelligible and intimidating as the figures he chalked on the board.

The bus lumbered out of the school parking lot, heading toward the foothills.

"Funny about that fire drill," Corey mused. "Mom was acting real paranoid this morning. She's afraid we're gonna have another brush-fire, like a few summers ago."

"My parents, too," Ericka said in surprise. "That fire was neat. Remember? It was right up there." She pointed to a far canyon.

Corey nodded. She and her mother had watched the flames from their living room window. Even though the fire burned miles away, Mrs. Johnson felt uneasy. Her husband was out of town, and she feared they'd have to evacuate. Corey had felt more excited than anything else. She remembered hoping the school would burn down so she'd have a longer vacation.

"Mom absolutely panicked," Ericka said. "She threw all our silverware and china in the swimming pool." A wry laugh. "The chlorine turned everything a pale green. Whoops—here's my stop." She slung her pack over one shoulder. "See you tonight. Come down as soon as you finish with Topher. And don't worry. You'll do fine."

"Right," Corey said, but her stomach said, *Wrong.* Why had she blurted to Ericka about telling Topher off? Now she had to go through with it, no matter how much her stomach disagreed.

Corey closed her eyes. Don't. Don't think about that. Concentrate on the road. She knew this area so well, she could envision each twist

30

and turn the bus would take.

Where were they now? Must be just past the Robles' house. Yes, she recognized that hairpin turn. Now they were nearing the Williamses'. She could smell the sweet jasmine bush in their front yard. Right about here was the eucalyptus tree Pete fell out of, breaking his arm. Coming up on the left, Topher's house. Strange. She didn't hear his cycle. He usually rode in the afternoon. And here—*clunk!* They were through the large pothole. Should be right in front of her house.

Corey opened her eyes. A blue sports car stood in the driveway. Pete was home!

She hurried off the bus and ran up the driveway, dry leaves scuttling across her path.

"Hey, Sis," Pete called affectionately. Clad only in a pair of faded Big Dogs, her brother lounged against his car, a hose in his hand. He gave Corey an unexpected hug.

"Want to cool off?" He gestured with the hose.

"Not that way," Corey said. "I want to hear all about school. Are the classes hard? Are you glad to be home?"

"Oh, yeah," Pete replied. He stretched luxuriously, his long arms reaching for the sky. "This weather's great. All we've had in Santa Cruz is fog. As for my classes, I spend hours, daily, slaving over a hot desk."

"Huh. Can't be too bad with Fridays off. I wish I had a three-day weekend every week."

"You'll be in college soon enough," Pete said.

Corey felt a tug at her heart. "Maybe," she said slowly. "Though I'm not sure I even want to go to college."

"What! Why not?"

"Oh, I don't know." Corey stared down at her sandals. "Sometimes I don't think I could ever leave home. I'd miss Mom and Dad, and the canyon, and Jabberwocky so much." She glanced up. Pete wore his concerned-brother expression. Reassured, Corey continued. "Pete, did you ever feel . . . sort of afraid and home-sick even before you went away? No, probably not. You're so much like Dad. So easygoing, taking everything in stride. Maybe I was adopted. Or maybe I was the milkman's baby. I'm the only one in this family that can't handle stuff."

"What do you mean 'stuff'?"

Corey made a helpless, circling gesture with her hands. "You know . . . changes."

"Corey," Pete said softly, "give yourself a little time. You don't have to be Miss Super I-Can-Adjust-to-Anything, before you're fifteen. Took me until I was—oh, at least eighteen before I became perfect."

"Dream on," Corey said, but she smiled.

Pete grinned as he sprayed the hood of his car. "Now tell me, how's high school going? Been scoping the older guys?"

Corey blushed. "*No*. How about you? Met any wonderful ladies?"

"A few."

"But none who measure up to your car?"

Pete aimed the hose at her. Corey moved quickly, laughing, away from the stream of water.

"No appreciation for a creature of true beauty," Pete said. He patted his car. "Run along, Sis. Gotta finish washing my baby here. There's bug juice all over her from the trip."

Corey skipped away, still smiling to herself. She turned once, just long enough to stick her tongue out at him. Pete returned the gesture, pleasantly.

"Mom! I'm home!" Corey grabbed a diet soda in the refrigerator, then went in search of her mother. Maybe she could clue her in on what had taken place between Topher and her dad.

The sign reading YES, I'M IN HERE hung on the darkroom door. Corey sighed. The sign was a gentle reminder that her mother was developing pictures and couldn't be disturbed. They'd have to talk later.

Upstairs in her room, Corey found Jabberwocky sprawled in his usual spot at the foot of the bed. When she tickled his belly, he nipped lightly at her fingers.

Corey gave a soft laugh. "Okay, I'm sorry. Just checking. She smoothed the fur on his head. "Guess you're feeling okay, huh?" She lay down on the bed, touching her nose to his. "Topher almost canceled you this morning with that cycle. And where would I be without you? Not even in kindergarden yet."

She pulled the cat to her and closed her eyes, thinking back ten years to her first day of school. She had felt so excited about starting kindergarden, about going to the same school as Pete. At least until that moment of icy panic when she stood nose-to-knob with the classroom door and realized her parents weren't coming in with her.

She had cried then, miserably, clinging to her mother's skirt. Only the promise of a kitten convinced her to take the teacher's outstretched hand. When she got home from school that afternoon, a quivering, complaining bit of fur awaited her.

"And I've loved you ever since," Corey said dreamily. The warm room closed around her, and she surrendered to the low, soothing sound of Jabberwocky's purr. A wind chime tinkled faintly outside. Corey fell into a sound sleep.

When she awoke, the room was dark.

"Corey!" her mother called. "Dinner!"

She sat up, feeling hot and groggy. The curtains billowed at her windows in a gust of Santa Ana. Her mother must've reopened the windows while she slept. It hadn't helped. Corey doubted the temperature had fallen much below ninety degrees.

Jabberwocky followed her to the bathroom where she washed her hands and splashed cool water on her face. Downstairs, she filled his bowl with dry food and joined her family.

"Corey, about this morning," her father began. "Did Topher talk with you at school?"

Again the stomach squeeze. Corey swallowed her mouthful of tuna-fish salad with difficulty.

"Well, sort of. He wanted to talk, but I—" She felt her cheeks burn. "I was busy. He's coming over tonight before I go to Ericka's."

"Oh, ho," Pete choked. "So you *are* scoping the older guys. A touch of the old 'boy next door' complex?"

"Pete, this is serious," Dr. Johnson said. He gestured at Corey with his fork. "I talked with Mrs. West about the incident this morning. She was most apologetic, and has grounded Topher. He can't ride his motorcycle for two weeks. And I asked him to apologize to you personally."

Corey felt as though she had dropped through the floor. Or suffered a heart attack. Or both. No wonder Topher wanted to speak to her alone. He was being forced to apologize! And grounded, too. Oh, he must hate her!

A shrill wail broke through her thoughts.

"Fire," Mrs. Johnson said uneasily. Another siren joined the first.

"Probably a false alarm," Dr. Johnson said. "Fire department's a little jumpy with the Santa Anas. High fire danger."

"Do you think we should stay home tonight?"

Dr. Johnson snorted. "Jan, are you kidding? And miss a party in an air-conditioned building?"

A horn honked outside.

"That's Greg," Pete said. He jumped up. "He's taking me to the football game tonight."

"You mean you're not taking your 'baby'?" Corey asked.

"No." Pete sounded shocked. "I just washed her. Gotta go."

Dr. Johnson pushed back his chair. "We'd better get going too, hon, or we'll be late."

"Corey, you've got cleanup duty tonight," her mother said.

"Okay."

The family dispersed. Corey put the food away, loaded the dishwasher, and hurried up to her room. The bedside clock said seven-thirty. Her heart gave a funny hop. Topher would be here any minute.

A soft knock on her door. "Bye, luv," Mrs. Johnson said, stepping in quickly. Corey thought her mother looked elegant. She wore a full-length, shimmery bronze cocktail dress and a pair of dangling diamond earrings.

"Have a good time at Ericka's," her mother continued. "And about you-know-who, firm but fair—hmmm?" She blew Corey a kiss.

Corey felt reassured by her mother's words. But when only a light scent of perfume lingered in the air, Corey grew doubtful again. Firm? *Ha!* She'd be lucky if she didn't cower in front of Topher.

She changed into a pair of shorts and a T-shirt, then packed a few things in her overnight bag. There. All ready for Ericka's. It was almost eight. Topher was probably keeping her waiting just to throw her off balance.

She sat down on the bed to wait. Eight-fifteen. She bit into a nail.

The phone rang.

Ericka, thought Corey. Wondering where I am.

"Why are you still there?" Ericka sounded concerned. "What did Topher say? I hope you let Jabberwocky bite him."

Corey sighed. "He's not even here yet. Ericka, I'm having second thoughts. Maybe I should just drop the whole thing. Let him say what he has to and forget the rest."

"What changed your mind?"

A short pause. Tears welled suddenly in Corey's eyes. "I can't stand up to him, Ericka. Even after what he did to Jabber. Topher was right from the start. I'm just a kid. A big chicken." She wiggled a finger in Jabber-wocky's face. "Here, Jab," she whispered. "Want a bite of wing?"

"Hey, Corey," Ericka said. "Whatever you decide, you know it's okay with me. Just hurry down here. Did you hear those sirens? There's some kind of—"

The line went dead.

An unexpected silence hung heavily in the hot evening air.

Santa Anas, Corey thought. Must've knocked down a phone line.

She replaced the receiver. Another siren screamed in the distance. The sound went through her body like a cold shiver.

Suddenly she was angry with Topher again. She wanted to get out of the house, away from the heat and the ominous feeling of doom that surrounded her. Only Topher was keeping her here. Well, she'd just march over to his house and talk to him *now*.

She grabbed her overnight bag and headed downstairs

Halfway down, the doorbell rang.

Here I come, Topher, Corey thought grimly. Ready or not.

CHAPTER
5

COREY SWUNG OPEN the front door. A gust of hot air blew against her, carrying a faint odor of smoke. The eucalyptus trees creaked in the wind, their dry leaves rustling together noisily. The porch was empty.

"Hey," a voice called. "Look at this."

Hesitantly, Corey peered out into the evening shadows. The sky seemed unusually bright. She could see the silhouette of a tall figure standing in the driveway.

"Who is it?" she asked. Her voice was uneasy.

"It's Topher," he snapped. "Who do you think?"

Corey walked toward him, her steps brisk with irritation.

"Well, how am I supposed to know it's you?" she replied defensively. "Maybe if you were at the front door instead of out here star-gazing, I—"

She stopped abruptly. With an impatient gesture, Topher pointed up to the distant hills.

Above several knolls arced a bright crimson halo. Its hot glow shimmered eerily through black shadows of smoke that rose to the sky.

"How far away do you think it is?" Topher asked.

Corey didn't answer. She forgot everything she had planned to say to him. She stood in frozen fascination, afraid to talk or move or breathe. The moment she did, the spell would break. The fire would become real.

Something fluttered down in front of her, lightly touching her on the cheek. Automatically, Corey opened her hand and caught several mothlike things in her palm.

No, not moths. *Ashes.*

Again she heard the scream of fire engines. Only this time they were closer. Her mother's words echoed around her. *One spark could start the whole neighborhood on fire.* Corey shivered.

Topher pulled at her arm. "How far away is it?" He repeated urgently.

"I—I'm not sure," she answered. "It's hard to tell with the trees. Might be in Coyote Canyon. That's only about a mile from here."

"Let's walk up the hill behind my house," Topher said. It was more of a command than a suggestion. "We can see better from there."

Corey nodded. "No, wait. I'll get a radio. The news should be on. Maybe it's just a small brushfire."

"Oh, sure," Topher said. "Just a small fire.

Going to barbecue a few hot dogs?"

Gravel sprayed under Corey's feet as she whirled to face him. Her words tumbled. "Look here, you don't know anything. I've lived here all my life. These brushfires are common. The fire department can handle it."

"Yeah?" Corey could detect scorn in his voice, yet he followed her into the house.

"That's weird," she said. She paused in the entryway. "I thought I left these lights on." She flicked the light switch. Nothing happened.

An icy panic crept through her veins. No power. The phones out, too.

"Do you have a flashlight?" Topher asked.

"I think my mom keeps one in the kitchen."

Slowly they groped their way through the dark house. Corey was glad Topher couldn't see her face. He mustn't know, mustn't see how frightened she was.

She opened a large kitchen drawer. Blindly, she touched bits of string, a scissors, tape. She sighed as her hand closed around the cool, metallic handle of the flashlight. Switching on its beam, she felt some of her composure return. The transistor radio lay in the corner of the same drawer.

"I hope the batteries are still good," Corey said. She dialed to her parents' favorite AM channel, which usually featured lots of evening news.

"I repeat," a disc jockey was saying, "fire and police officials ask that you stay out of the

41

area. The blaze has been declared out of control, and many residents of Coyote and Sycamore canyons are being evacuated. We'll bring you more details as they become available."

Corey's panic deepened. She glanced at Topher. His face seemed as cold and tight as always. Yet there was a look of uncertainty in his eyes.

"Where are your parents?" he asked.

"At a party." Her voice trembled.

"My mom's at work," Topher explained. "Night shift at the hospital. She's a nurse."

Corey nodded mutely. There was no one to help them.

"Come on. We can't just stand here," Topher said "I want a better look at this fire. Then we'll know if we're in any danger."

Corey followed him outside, still clutching the radio.

Together they trudged up the steep road behind their homes. The air was hot, and Corey found it difficult to breathe. Wild gusts of Santa Anas tugged at her constantly. She stumbled once, but Topher caught her with a strong arm. "Thanks," she mumbled, a blush creeping to her cheeks. Topher didn't seem to hear. The roaring wind drowned out her words and those of the disc jockey, still broadcasting over the radio. Corey tried to grasp the fragments of news she heard. " . . . cause is yet undetermined . . . gusts up to sixty miles an hour . . . at least twenty homes threatened . . . Red Cross stations set up for evacuees . . ."

At last they reached the top of the hill. Corey pushed her wind-whipped hair from her eyes and looked down over the other side.

Her mouth opened in horror. The canyon was an ocean of orange flame. How had it spread so fast? The blaze leaped frantically like stormy surf, engulfing brush and trees. Hot embers and acrid smoke brew up into her face. Corey's eyes smarted with tears.

"Let's get out of here!" she cried. She had to scream for Topher to hear. The crackling sound of the flames was deafening.

Quickly they moved back from the crest of the hill.

"What do we do now?" Topher asked. His blue eyes were wide. He seemed to be looking to her for guidance.

"I don't know," Corey said. Her voice fell to a whisper. "I don't know . . ." Her first instinct was to run, to hide. Then her gaze fell upon her house. It lay nestled, vulnerable at the base of the canyon, its windows dark and blind to the fire.

The flames raged closer. Soon they would reach her home. Her home! She had to save it.

Corey took a deep breath. She turned to Topher and spoke rapidly.

"Close all the windows in your house. That'll keep embers from blowing inside. Get a hose and water down your roof. We can hold the flames back until the fire department comes. Hurry!"

Topher gave a curt nod. They separated.

Corey's heart pounded wildly, propelling her down the hill toward her house. This time she didn't need the flashlight inside. The rooms were lit with the eerie glow of flames. The fire had reached the top of the hill.

She hurried from room to room, slamming window after window. So many stupid windows, she thought. All of them open. Stupid Santa Anas!

In one of the rooms, she misplaced the radio. Precious minutes were lost as she backtracked to find it. Finding that radio seemed the most important thing in her life. The phones were dead. No way to reach her parents. The radio was her only outside contact.

Corey searched frantically. "This is dumb," she finally said aloud. Who cared about the radio? The fire was getting closer.

She ran outside again to get the garden hose. Her fingers trembled as she fumbled to connect it to the spigot. "Come on!" Corey panted. "Hurry!" At last it twisted into place. She turned the water on full force. The hose gurgled, but only a tiny stream of water trickled out.

Corey's heart turned cold. She looked up. The fire moved swiftly down through the dry weeds. Leaves and large pieces of bark fell burning onto the grass. Corey tried to stamp out the burning patches with her feet. She grabbed the welcome mat from the front porch and brought it down again and again, fiercely attacking the flames.

Topher appeared beside her, his face smudged black. Damp curls clung to his forehead with perspiration.

"Give it up," he said. "We gotta leave."

"No." Corey's voice as hoarse with emotion. "Wait for the fire department. They'll be here soon."

"You stupid kid," Topher said. "Nobody's coming. This fire's out of control."

"I have to save it. It's my house. Don't you understand?"

"It's too late," Topher said. "Look!"

Corey tore her gaze away from the fear she saw in Topher's cold blue eyes. A corner of the roof was on fire. Dry shingles crackled and burst into tiny explosions of flame.

Her shoulders sagged.

"I've got my motorcycle. Let's go." Topher grabbed her arm, pulling her away from the house.

"Wait," Corey cried. "Jabberwocky! Jabber's still inside."

She shook off Topher's hand and raced back into the house, bounding the stairs three at a time. Flame shadows danced on the walls of her room.

"Jabber," she called. "Jabber! C'mon, baby." Where was he? Not in his usual spot.

Frantically, she looked in her closet, behind the bureau. "Jabber!" She found him at last, huddled far beneath the bed.

No time for gentle coaxing now. She dragged him from his hiding spot. His claws snagged on the carpet. Holding him tightly, Corey glanced around the room. What else should she take? Books? Clothes? That picture of her and Ericka? Everything was important. Everything seemed to scream, *Take me with you, don't leave me behind.* She couldn't choose. It was bad luck. If she took something, it meant she'd never be back. And she would be back. She would!

She ran from the room.

Outside, the pungent odor of burning eucalyptus assaulted Corey's nose. She sneezed violently. Her eyes watered and she stopped short, trying to see through the smoke and tears. Topher waited for her at the edge of the driveway.

"Hurry! Over here!" he ordered.

Corey raced toward him.

She was almost hit by the large tree limb that fell burning across her path. Jabberwocky struggled in her grasp and she cried out as his claws dug into her chest. For a second, she loosened her hold. Claws slashed down her stomach as the cat leaped from her arms. He darted back to the house.

"Jabberwocky!" Corey screamed. She moved to go after him, but Topher held her back.

"It's too late," he said, his voice flat.

"No—No—No!" Corey tried to run. Topher shook her, his hands gripping, hurting her arms.

"Stop it!" he yelled. "We've got to get out of here. If we don't, we'll die!" He shook her again. "Do you hear me?"

Corey nodded. Topher kicked the starter and she heard the familiar growl as his cycle came to life.

"Get on. Hold on tight," Topher said.

Corey wrapped her arms around his waist and buried her face into the back of his T-shirt. It smelled of smoke and sweat. Then the motorcycle lurched forward and she felt the wind in her ears as they roared down the canyon road.

CHAPTER
6

COREY FELT AS IF SHE were hurtling down a deep hole. Hot, stifling winds whipped against her, thrashing her hair. Her stomach pitched as the motorcycle swayed around each corner. Questions reeled in her mind. How could she find her parents? Would the fire department reach her house? Was Jabberwocky dead?

Oh, please. Don't let him be dead—

The motorcycle slowed.

"Why are we stopping?" Corey yelled. Unconsciously, she tightened her grip around Topher's waist, squeezing in apprehension.

"Traffic jam," Topher said.

"What?" Corey peered nervously over his shoulder. Her breath caught in astonishment.

People, dozens of people, congested the road ahead. They hurried from their homes, shouting, calling to each other, arms laden with clothes and belongings or wide-eyed children.

Cars honked impatiently and crawled forward, anxious to join the endless train of refugees. Above them all, against the red sky, eucalyptus trees bowed awkwardly in the approaching fire wind.

"Where—where's everyone going?" Corey asked.

Topher shrugged. "Don't know. They're just leaving. Like us."

A cold lump lodged in Corey's throat. Until this moment, she had felt totally alone. Now she realized other homes, other people, were in danger, too.

But these weren't just other people, she thought suddenly. They were the Robleses. The Williamses. *Friends.*

Ericka. Her home was threatened, too.

The lump in Corey's throat hardened. She felt as if she had swallowed an ice cube. Tears burned behind her eyes, but she couldn't cry. The ice cube wouldn't melt. Dry-eyed and disbelieving, she stared at the chaotic scene around her.

A soft tap on her shoulder. Corey looked up. Her mind slowly registered the black uniform, the hat, the badge.

"Keep moving, kids," the policeman said. He motioned with a bullhorn. "We've got to evacuate this area immediately."

Topher started to argue, but the policeman moved away.

"Welcome to the Los Angeles freeway,"

Topher muttered. "At rush hour." He gestured in annoyance. "How are we supposed to keep moving if no one else is? I've seen snails jog faster." Slowly, he nosed the cycle forward. "Is that cop looking this way?"

Corey scanned the crowd. "No."

"Good. I don't want him to see this."

The cycle lurched. Corey grabbed for Topher's waist.

"Hey!" she cried. "What are you doing?"

Topher didn't answer. They sped down the center of the road, Topher recklessly dodging people and weaving through the stream of cars. Dogs barked. Kids yelled. Once, they nearly sideswiped an old man carrying a bird cage. The man cursed loudly, and Corey could hear the bird squawking as they flew past. Fear and anger surged inside her.

"Are you nuts?" she screamed into Topher's ear. "You're gonna kill somebody. Like us!"

Topher turned his head and glared at her for a split second. "It's a long walk to the bottom of the canyon," he threatened.

Corey gripped his waist even tighter.

"Not so hard!"

"Sorry," Corey said, though she wasn't. If Topher was going to drive like a maniac, she'd have to hold on like one.

The canyon road seemed to twist on forever, but at last they turned the final bend. Several police cars blocked the intersection ahead, their red lights flashing. A crowd of anxious people argued and pleaded with police officers standing nearby. To avoid the confusion, Topher pulled around the roadblock into the dirt.

"Wait, stop!" Corey cried. "I think I see my parents. There's Pete!"

Before Topher could bring the cycle to a complete stop, Corey leaped off the back. She stumbled into the crowd, her legs weak and unsteady. Police lights flashed and blinded her. She stood still, confused.

Where were they? She knew she had seen them. Where . . . ?

Her eyes focused again.

There.

"Mom! Dad!" She ran into her father's arms.

"We were so worried," he said.

"I'm okay, I'm okay." Corey buried her head in his shirt. She breathed the comforting smell of his aftershave. Yes, everything was okay now. Mom and Dad would take care of everything. Just as always.

"We were so worried," her father repeated. "Pete came to the party, told us about the fire. We tried to phone you at Ericka's. The Smiths were getting ready to evacuate. Ericka said you'd never arrived—" His voice broke. Corey looked up into his eyes and saw a glisten of tears.

"The police wouldn't let us up to the house in the car," Mrs. Johnson said. "The whole area's blocked off. Dad was just about to walk up and find you." Tentatively, she touched

Corey's head. "Are you all right? What about the house?"

"We've got to go back," Corey said hurriedly. She couldn't tell her mother about seeing the flames on the roof. "If we get help, I'm sure we can save the house. And Jabberwocky's up there. We've got to get him."

Pete squeezed her hand. He'd lost his usual nonchalance. "Glad you're okay, Sis. We could see the fire from the football stadium. They stopped the game. Corey, what about my car? Dad, I want to go get it."

"I'll go with you," Corey said. "Jabberwocky—"

"No. Absolutely not." Dr. Johnson's voice was hard, almost angry. "I thought we'd lost Corey. I won't risk losing both of you. The best thing now is to stay out of the way and let the fire crews do their jobs. We'll get Pete's car and Jabberwocky in the morning." He paused, then smiled grimly. "We'll check into a nice motel by the beach. Your mother always claims Santa Barbara would be a good place for a vacation."

"This isn't what I had in mind," Mrs. Johnson said, but she smiled and took her husband's arm.

Reluctantly, Corey followed her family through the crowd to the car.

"Wait. What about Topher?" she asked. "I forgot all about him."

"Topher?" Mrs. Johnson's eyebrows arched in surprise. "Was he with you?"

"Yes. We came down the canyon on his motorcycle. I've got to thank him."

Corey ran back to the spot where she had left Topher. He was gone.

Just as well, she thought. He would have laughed at her, or said something rude, as usual. With good reason, too. She'd been so scared, she had squeezed him like a boa constrictor all the way down the hill. Her cheeks flushed. Good grief! She could never face him again.

"Did you find him?" her mother asked.

Corey shook her head and scooted into the car.

No one said a word during the ride through town. The silence in the car made her feel as if they were driving to a funeral. They pulled up in front of a motel and sat while Dr. Johnson went inside to get them a room.

A few minutes later, the Johnsons checked into a two-bedroom suite. Corey sank, exhausted, into a chair that faced a sliding-glass door and the balcony beyond. A view of the mountains filled her eyes. Flames jerked and twitched almost comically, like the actors in an old-time movie. Corey leaped up and closed the curtains with a fierce yank.

"Why couldn't we get a room with a view of the beach?" she asked.

Dr. Johnson came out of the bathroom carrying an ice bucket. "All sold out," he answered. "Jan, do you want a Coke or Seven-Up?"

"Seven-Up, please."

"Pete?"

"Coke. Two of 'em."

"Corey?"

"No. Nothing, thanks."

Corey watched her father disappear out the door, presumably heading for the soda machine. Then she began to wander restlessly about the room, straightening a picture, poking in closets, peering into the mini-refrigerator in the kitchenette.

"Corey, please settle down," her mother said in a mild voice.

Corey stared at her. Mrs. Johnson, who usually hated to sit idle, lay curled on the double bed, listening to fire reports on the radio. Pete sat down a foot from the television, engrossed in a "Twilight Zone" episode. Just then, Dr. Johnson came back, the ice bucket filled with frosty cans of soda.

"Isn't this great?" he said. "No luggage to hassle with, no bellhops to tip. The only way to travel."

"What's wrong with you guys?" Corey blurted. "I mean, you're acting like nothing's wrong, like nothing's happened. Shouldn't we be *doing* something? We can't just sit here!"

Her father shrugged in a helpless gesture. "Honey, there's nothing else we can do. Not right now."

"Why don't you take a shower," Mrs. Johnson suggested absently. "Or go to bed. You've had a rough evening."

Corey felt a stab of loneliness. She longed to have her father's arms around her again, or to hear her mother's usual firm, reassuring words. But her parents and Pete seemed to have forgotten her. Corey wandered outside, sliding the door shut softly behind her. Clutching the balcony rail, she looked up at the hills. They glowed so brightly, she imagined she could feel the heat from the flames.

The sound of voices startled her. She had thought she was alone. A few guests stood nearby, watching from their balconies. They talked loudly, their voices carrying.

"Isn't it awful?"

"The sky—it's so frightening it's almost beautiful."

" . . . might burn the whole town."

" . . . last reports, over fifty homes burned."

"All those homeless people! Think how they must feel!"

I'm one of those people, Corey thought, stunned. But she didn't feel anything. Nothing except a numbing emptiness. There must be something wrong with her. Her house could be burning down. Shouldn't she feel something more?

A hot gust of wind blew full into her face. Her premonition that morning had been right. Something awful *had* been waiting to happen to her. And the Santa Anas had brought it.

CHAPTER
7

COREY STABBED A FORKFUL of pancakes and swirled it listlessly in the thick syrup on her plate.

Let's try this again, she thought. She knew she had to eat.

She brought the fork up to her mouth. The next instant, it clattered to the plate as her stomach flipped in warning.

"Are you all right?" her mother asked.

Corey looked up and smiled weakly across the table. "Sure." Actually, her head ached and her eyes felt puffed and itchy. She vaguely remembered tumbling into bed only a few hours before. The official word had come at five in the morning: the fire was contained.

"You look like you just staggered home after one of Ericka's wild slumber parties," Mrs. Johnson remarked. Her forced smile couldn't hide the strained look on her face. "Of course, I'm not one to talk. I'm a bit overdressed for this coffee shop. Especially at ten in the morning."

The bronze-colored cocktail dress slowly registered in Corey's mind. Funny, she hadn't noticed her mother was still wearing it. But of course she would. What else did she have to wear?

Corey glanced down at her own clothes. They were smudged black and reeked of smoke. Bloodstains dotted the front of her T-shirt. She touched them with light fingers and winced. The scratches underneath were tight and sore.

Jabberwocky!

Mrs. Johnson took a sip of coffee. Her hands trembled. "I wish your dad would get here," she said. "I hate this waiting, not knowing anything for sure."

At eight that morning, fire officials had announced that residents could return to the fire area. Dr. Johnson and Pete had left immediately to check on the house, promising to meet Corey and her mother in the coffee shop at ten.

"Here they come now," Corey said. She tried to guess her father's news, but his expression was closed.

Pete sat heavily in the seat next to her. Dr. Johnson gently took his wife's hands in his own as he slid into the booth beside her. He drew a long breath.

"The house is gone," he said bluntly. "I'm— sorry."

Corey swallowed with difficulty. The ice cube grew colder.

"Isn't anything left?" Mrs. Johnson asked.

57

Her eyes looked tired and pleading. "Some furniture? The china? My photographs—what about my photographs?"

Her husband's voice was expressionless. "The house burned to the ground, Jan. The fire was very hot. Nothing's left. It's all rubble."

"What about Ericka's house?" Corey asked.

"I don't remember seeing it, so I guess it's gone, too. The whole neighborhood was leveled. The morning paper says two hundred homes burned last night."

Two hundred homes! Corey's mind reeled. It might well have been two million. Both figures were too outrageous to comprehend.

Tears spilled down Mrs. Johnson's cheeks. "When I think of the years we struggled to afford that house. Corey and Pete were born there. It was our first real home. All the baby pictures, my wedding gown, everything, gone . . ." Her voice trailed off. With a sob, she turned to her husband. He held her, patting her trembling shoulders.

Corey sat looking at her hands. *Everything, gone.* . . . Fourteen years, her whole life. All torn away from her, destroyed in a few hours. This couldn't be happening. None of it was real.

A twinge of pain. Corey jerked suddenly, remembering. "Dad, what about Jabberwocky? Did you see him?"

Pete spoke for the first time. "You and that cat." His voice was ragged, angry. "Is that all you can think about? You should see my car.

It's burnt to a crisp. Why didn't you drive it out? Too busy joy riding around with that jerk Topher?"

Corey's lips quivered. Her brother's words stung.

"Pete, you know I don't know how to drive!"

"Well, you could've taken the trouble to save something. You were the only one home. You were responsible."

"That's enough, Pete," Dr. Johnson said.

Pete seemed not to hear. "What were you doing there all that time? Was your brain turned off?"

"There wasn't time," Corey whispered, her throat tightening. "You don't know. You weren't there. There wasn't time to do anything. I tried to save the house."

A sharp laugh. "Sure, fat chance of that. You couldn't even save your stupid cat."

"Peter!" Dr. Johnson's voice exploded in the restaurant. Several people turned and stared. A waitress hurried over, pen and pad in her hand.

"Is everything all right, sir?" she asked. "Are you ready to order?"

"No!" Dr. Johnson shouted.

The waitress turned and fled.

"Way to go, Dad," Pete said.

Dr. Johnson spoke quietly now. "I'm sorry. I didn't mean to lose my temper. We can't tear each other apart over this. Pete, Corey did her best. Now we have to do ours." He ran his fingers through his dark hair. "We have to stick together. Do you understand?"

Pete said nothing. He sat twisting a napkin between his fingers.

"Your dad's right," Mrs. Johnson said. She blotted her swollen eyes with a soggy tissue. "We still have each other. We'll be—okay, if we work together as a family."

"This is bull." Pete stood up. "I can't listen to any more. I'm going back to the motel." He threw the napkin on the table and was gone before anyone could stop him.

"Dad," Corey said miserably, "I tried to save the house. Honest."

Her father reached out, touching her hand. "I know, honey. Pete's just upset. I'm proud of what you tried to do. But a fire of that intensity isn't something you fool with. It's too unpredictable. You did right, leaving when you did. The paper said several people were burned seriously, trying to save their homes." He looked straight into her eyes. "Our house isn't worth you getting hurt—"

Corey nodded. Her father patted her hand and smiled. It was a strained smile, yet Corey felt a little warmth seep into her.

"Dad," she said again, "what about Jabber? I want to go up and see the house, what's left of it, and look for him."

Dr. Johnson shook his head. "Not today, Corey. We have too much to do."

The warmth faded. "But, Dad—"

"You can look later, Corey," her mother said. "I'm sure Jab's okay. If he can outrun Topher's cycle, no fire can catch him."

"Mom, Dad, you don't understand." Corey gestured in frustration. "Jabber ran back to the house and it was burning. I—"

Dr. Johnson held up his hand. "Corey, please. We don't have time for this now. And I don't want your mother upset with morbid details, so let's drop the subject." He turned to his wife. "Jan, do you have a pen in your purse?" She handed one to him, and he began making notes on a paper napkin. "I'll try to contact the insurance company. See what our next step should be. I'll drop you and Corey at the mall. Pick up a few necessities for us. Toothbrushes, underwear, any clothes you think we'll need right away . . ."

Dr. Johnson's voice droned on. Corey picked up her fork and plunged the pancakes into the lake of syrup. She imagined they were animals, drowning, their ears filling with the sticky sweetness so they couldn't hear, so she couldn't hear. She couldn't listen to Dad anymore. Couldn't watch him plan their lives on a stupid paper napkin. She wanted to talk. About the fire, and Jabber. About the strange sense of unreality she felt about everyone and everything.

Corey sighed. If only there were some way to reach Ericka. But Ericka's family could be staying at one of any number of motels in

Santa Barbara . . .

Three hours later, Corey stood in a dressing room at Sears. Her thoughts of Ericka persisted. Maybe Mom would take her to the Smiths' property when they finished shopping. *If* they ever finished. There was so much to buy. At this rate, they'd have to celebrate Christmas on the Sears escalator.

Corey tucked a green plaid blouse into the stiff new jeans she wore. Perfect fit. Big deal. Who cared about shopping now? She'd give anything to have a few old clothes. Just one pair of old Reeboks instead of these dumb sandals. Or maybe the gold necklace Ericka had given her for her birthday. Even that old pink sweater she hated.

"Corey?" Her mother's voice.

"Here, Mom. In this stall."

Mrs. Johnson's head appeared in the dressing room.

"Those jeans look nice," she said. "You may get them if you like. Lucky I had my charge cards with me last night, although we'll have to watch our finances carefully for a while. I don't know how much money we'll get from the insurance company."

Corey began to undress.

"Stay in your jeans," her mother said. "I explained our situation to the saleswoman. We can wear a new outfit home."

Corey sighed with relief. All morning long, she had felt self-conscious in her smoky clothes. Salespeople and customers had stared at them, pointing or whispering, shaking their heads in sympathy. Her mother, acting briefly like herself again, ignored the stares, sailing nonchalantly through the store as if she always shopped for underwear in an expensive evening gown. But Corey had only cringed with embarrassment. Strangers pitying her made her feel low and poor and dirty.

When they got to the car, Corey said, "Mom, do you think we could go up to the house now? Just for a little while? I promise, we don't have to stay long."

Mrs. Johnson bit her lip and was silent for a minute. "I just can't, Corey," she said at last. "I can't face it. I don't want to see what's left of our house, remembering the way it used to be." She took a tissue from her purse and wiped quickly at her eyes. I doubt if I'll ever go up to the canyon again."

"Mom!" Corey couldn't believe her ears. "Mom, you can't mean that. It's still our— home, isn't it? Mom, Ericka might be there. And Jabberwocky." When her mother didn't respond, she said, "I keep thinking that if I see it, see everything burned, that I'll finally believe it happened. That it's real."

"It's all too real for me," her mother said, her voice bitter.

"Well, fine," Corey said defiantly. "If you won't drive me, I'll ask Dad. He'll take me up to the house right away. I know he will."

But when they returned to the motel, Corey found her father arguing with someone on the phone.

The insurance company. When her father got off the line, he would be in no mood to listen to her pleas.

Feeling lost and discouraged, Corey wandered down to the motel pool. The Santa Anas had abated with the fire, but the weather remained warm. Corey gazed at the sky. A deep, fantasy blue. Strange that it could look so beautiful the day after a disaster.

She saw Pete lying on a lounge chair, his back to the mountains. He still wore the same shorts from the day before. Corey approached him hesitantly, afraid he might yell at her again.

"Hi," she said. "Sunbathing, huh? Mind if I sit here?"

"You're blocking my sun," Pete said simply, his voice hard.

"Oh. Sorry." She pulled up a chair beside him. An awkward silence.

"What have you been doing all day?" Corey asked finally.

Pete didn't look at her. "Nothing."

"Mom and I got you a couple of shirts and some jeans."

Another silence.

Talk to me, Corey thought. Please, talk to me. Be my brother again.

"Pete, is everything really gone? What did

the house look like? Tell me, please."

"I don't want to talk about it."

Corey nibbled a fingernail. "Pete, I know you're mad about your car and everything, but could you help me talk to Mom and Dad? Get them to take me to the canyon? They'll listen to you, Pete. See, I have to go up there. I have to find Jabberwocky—" She stopped.

Pete turned his head and stared coldly at her for a long moment. Where had she seen another look like that? Eyes filled with pain and bitterness.

"Just leave me alone," Pete said evenly. He turned away.

Corey didn't move. She sat numbly, hands in her lap, like a scolded child.

Pete hated her. He'd probably never speak to her again. What would she do without his easy, teasing support? With him and her parents acting so strange, who could she turn to, talk to?

She stood and walked slowly back to the motel room. She had so many questions, and not one single person to answer them.

CHAPTER
8

COREY AWAKENED but did not open her eyes.

If she kept them closed, she could still be at home in her own room. She could smell the tangy scent of canyon sage coming through we open window. Jabberwocky was sleeping at the bottom of her bed. In a minute, Topher would start up his cycle and she—

Corey opened her eyes.

The fantasy crumbled. Four motel walls stared down at her. She sighed. Seven-thirty Monday morning: time to get up for school.

"You don't have to go," her father had said the night before. "The fire's a reasonable excuse to take a few days off."

Corey nodded. "I know, Dad. But Pete went back to school. Why shouldn't I?"

Dr. Johnson fell silent then, a hint of worry in his eyes.

Corey felt a stab of guilt. She shouldn't

have mentioned Pete. After her poolside conversation with him on Saturday, he'd hardly said a word to anyone. When questioned, he answered in a lifeless voice, and his face took on a closed, sullen appearance. On Sunday afternoon, he suddenly, angrily, announced that he wanted to return to Santa Cruz. Their parents drove him to the bus station without comment, though Corey suspected they were worried about his behavior.

She was, too. Okay, so maybe he hated her. So maybe he still blamed her for the fate of his car. She could understand that. But if he was angry, why didn't he scream and yell and tell her off? Anything would be better than his cold, strange silence. When he left town, he didn't even tell her good-bye.

"Honestly, Dad," Corey had continued. "If Mom doesn't need me for anything, I'd like to go to school. I'll fall behind in my classes if I don't." She was surprised at how convincing her argument sounded. Actually, she didn't care one bit about her classes. She only wanted to be someplace where there was some kind of order and routine. All weekend she had felt upside-down, like Alice falling through the rabbit hole into Wonderland. Everyone acted so weird. Pete, with his quiet anger. Dad, making lists of things to do. Mom, chatting away one moment, sobbing the next.

Worst of all, Corey thought, there's me. She felt so alone. Even sitting in the same room as her parents, she felt as if they hardly noticed her presence. Did they know or care that she was hurting, too? Maybe. But she couldn't talk to them anymore. They were strangers. Only Ericka could help, and school would make things seem normal again.

"Try to have a good day, honey," Mrs. Johnson said as she dropped Corey off in front of the high school. "Remember, I'll pick you up at three. If you want to come back to the motel early, just call."

Corey watched her mother drive away, then walked slowly to her locker. She felt self-conscious in her new clothes. No one seemed to notice. Kids pushed past her, hurrying, laughing, calling to one another.

Mechanically, she spun the combination of her locker. The door sprung open. Corey gave a small cry of surprise.

Her old pink sweater. It was stuffed in behind her history book, one sleeve peeking out. She had always hated this sweater. It made her itch and the color clashed with her hair. She had brought it to school a few weeks ago, to give to Ericka, and then forgotten all about it.

Now she pulled it out, crushing it between her fingers. The prickly yarn tickled her. How could she have hated it? It was the most beautiful sweater in the world, the only sweater left from the "before" time. Before the fire, before life changed. Only three days ago!

"Corey?"

She whirled at the familiar voice.

"Ericka!" Corey hugged her friend, almost wanting to laugh. "Ericka, I'm so glad to see you!"

"Me, too! I mean, I'm glad to see *you*. I mean . . . Oh, Corey, I've been so worried! I didn't know how to reach you, and I didn't think you'd be back at school this soon." Ericka touched Corey's arm. "Are you okay? I'm really sorry about your house."

Corey smiled and hugged her friend again. Mmmm, coconut perfume. Good old Ericka. She never changed, even in the face of disaster.

"I wanted to talk to you so bad this weekend," Corey said. "Our whole neighborhood gone. Doesn't seem real, does it? Where are you staying? I didn't know where to call you, either."

"What do you mean?"

"We're at the Playa Azul Motel," Corey said. "Are you at a motel, too?"

"I—we're home, Corey. Didn't you know? Our house was one of the few that didn't burn. I thought you knew."

Corey shut her locker. The metallic clang sounded a hollow echo deep inside her. "No, I didn't know. Dad said he thought your house burned."

"It should've. One part of the roof caught fire. Corey, it was awful! Dad made Mom take us girls to Grandma's, down in L.A. But he wouldn't leave." Ericka spoke rapidly, as if trying to avoid reliving the scene. "I guess Dad flagged down a couple of firefighters. They used a special machine to pump water out of our pool and onto the house. Dad's fruit trees are totaled, but we'll only have to replace a few shingles on the roof. We were lucky."

Corey couldn't believe her words. Ericka's house—saved! She heard herself mumbling all the correct things. *Happy you're all right, Ericka. Glad about your house.* But even as she spoke she knew she wasn't glad at all. She felt horribly betrayed. Why had her house burned and not Ericka's? It wasn't fair!

"There goes the bell," Corey said. "You'd better hurry. If you're late to algebra once more, Yenke will kill you."

"Who cares?" Ericka replied. "I want to talk to you. Find out how you are, how your family is."

"At lunch, okay?" Corey started to back away.

Ericka frowned slightly. "Well, sure. Our usual spot."

"Great. See you." Before her friend could reply, Corey slipped away into the jostling crowd of students. If she had stood there one millisecond more, Ericka would've been able to read the flushed guilt on her face. She had no intention of talking to Ericka at lunch. Maybe not ever.

Ericka's house hadn't burned. Her friend

70

wouldn't, couldn't understand. Corey felt more alone than ever.

The feeling persisted as the morning shuffled by. Pointless to come to school, she thought miserably. None of the normal activity she sought was here. The routines, the schedules, only made her aware that she was set apart now, even more than before.

Corey moved from class to class like a sleepwalker, sitting with the rest of the students, yet feeling invisible. She tried to listen to the lectures, automatically jotting notes, but the teachers' words and the words on her paper seemed alien. Nothing made sense. Unreality surrounded her like a long, glass tunnel. She could see, but couldn't reach, the end.

Have to get out, she thought, suddenly panicked. The tunnel moved in around her, closer and closer. Sweat gathered on her forehead.

Have to escape. Now.

The noon bell rang. Corey almost tripped hurrying to the door.

"Can I see you a moment, Corey? Corey?"

Her name. Someone was calling her name.

Corey pulled herself back into the classroom. Students pushed past her into the hall. Miss Winkler, her lit teacher, beckoned to her, a kind smile on her face.

"I read about your house," the teacher said. She placed her hands gently on Corey's shoulders. "I'm so sorry."

"How did you—?" Corey began, then stopped. The Sunday paper had printed a list of families whose homes had burned. Miss Winkler must have recognized her father's name.

Miss Winkler gave Corey's shoulder a little squeeze. "If there's anything I can do . . ."

"No, no thanks," Corey said. She backed away, her breath coming in short gasps. The glass tunnel was closing in. "Thanks, but— I've gotta go. Please."

Out in the hall, she felt a little better. She took several deep breaths. Odd, this hot, panicky feeling. And why had she run from Miss Winkler? The teacher had only wanted to help.

Corey closed her eyes. Miss Winkler was nice, but that kind of help wouldn't make a difference. She needed someone who could understand. *Really* understand.

Sensing someone watching her, Corey glanced up. Across the hall, Topher lounged against a row of lockers. He wore the same smoke-stained jeans he'd had on Friday night, but his black T-shirt was new. The face of Bruce Springsteen, silk-screened in blue on the front, still bore creases from package folds. Topher gazed at her intently. He seemed to be waiting. Waiting for her.

Corey pressed her books tightly against her stomach, trying to quell the familiar elephant hops. "Hi," she said finally.

72

Topher lifted his chin slightly in acknowledgment.

"I forget to thank you for the other night," Corey continued. She cleared her throat. "I looked for you after I found my parents, but you'd left."

A short silence.

Topher pushed his hands into his pockets. He glanced down the hall, one corner of his mouth curling in contempt. "I didn't want to intrude," he said. "It was such a tender scene, you know. You and your family. The Great Reunion."

"Why do you always say things like that?" Corey demanded. When he didn't answer, she turned away. Good. She was glad he'd made her mad. It relieved her nervousness—and any obligation she'd felt to thank him.

"Good-bye," she said coldly. She had walked only a few feet when she heard Topher following. His motocross boots echoed heavily in the hallway.

"Have you been up to the canyon yet?" he asked.

"No." Corey kept walking. She didn't look at him.

"I have. It's unreal. Ever see those pictures of England and Germany after World War Two? Looks just like that." Topher gave a long whistle. "Bombed. Nothing left standing except the chimneys."

"I—I'd like to see it," Corey said slowly.

"Not because I'm morbid. I just need to see it. My dad keeps saying we don't have time or it's too dangerous. But I want to go. My cat is—" She stopped. She didn't want to mention Jabberwocky, especially to Topher.

"Where are you staying?" Topher asked.

"Playa Azul Motel. Where are you staying? With friends?"

"No, a small motel on upper State Street. It's a real dive, but the best my mom can afford right now. We don't have much insurance. I don't know what's gonna happen when the money runs out."

They walked together out the main doors. Corey blinked in the sunshine.

"Look," Topher said suddenly, "if you want to go up to the canyon, I can take you on my bike." A bitter smile. "I'm not grounded anymore."

Corey said nothing. She felt torn between telling him how desperately she wanted to go and telling him exactly where *he* should go.

"How about it?"

"Why are you being so nice to me all of a sudden?" Corey asked.

"Maybe I'm not," Topher replied. "You haven't seen the canyon yet. Want to go or not?"

"After school?"

"No. Now."

Corey stopped walking. "You mean cut class?"

"'You mean cut class?'" Topher mimicked

74

her, adding a high, unflattering tone to his voice. "Why not? Can you see any reason to stay here?" He waved his hand. "All this seems so—so stupid compared to what you'll see in the canyon. Besides," he added, "cutting is no sweat. I do it all the time."

"I don't know," Corey said. "What do I use for an excuse tomorrow?"

"Plead temporary insanity. You're still shook about the fire. No one will hassle you."

Corey chewed her lower lip.

"What's the matter," Topher said. "Scared?"

Scared. Corey turned the word over in her mind. No, she wasn't scared to cut class. But she was scared about how she'd feel, how she'd react when she'd see the charred rubble, all that remained of her home. Now that she had the chance, she wasn't sure she wanted to see the canyon, wasn't sure that it was worth it.

Then she remembered Jabberwocky.

"No, I'm not afraid," she told Topher. "Let's go."

CHAPTER
9

"HURRY UP," TOPHER SAID. He revved the motorcycle impatiently. "Somebody might see us."

As nonchalantly as possible, Corey swung her leg over the seat behind him.

It'll be okay, she told herself. You won't get caught. Then she imagined her mother wailing, *My daughter, cutting class! She was always such a good girl! Where did I go wrong?*

Her stomach fell away as the cycle jerked forward. She grabbed Topher's waist, her whole body tense.

Here we go again. Who gave this guy driving lessons, a kangaroo?

"Just relax," Topher called back to her. "Don't fight it. Sway with the bike."

"Sure, then I fall off," Corey muttered. But she tried leaning with the bike through the next corner, and to her surprise, it worked.

This motorcycle stuff isn't so bad, she realized after the first couple of miles. Noisy. Definitely noisy. She looked over her shoulder and saw the street rushing beneath them like a river. She glanced away. Scary, too. Yet there was something exhilarating about being frightened, about cutting through the air without the protection of a car surrounding her.

Corey shook her head, letting the cool wind catch her hair. She felt more alive than she had in days.

They soon reached the intersection at the base of the canyon. Topher passed it, and the engine complained as they turned up the steep side street.

"Where are we going?" Corey shouted into the wind.

"Gotta take the back way into the foothills," Topher answered. "Fire crews are still clearing the main roads. This other route didn't burn."

Corey nodded. They rode in silence.

At the back entrance, a uniformed man motioned for them to stop. The road was blocked by three large sawhorses.

"National Guard," the man said. "I need to see some identification. Only residents allowed in the fire area."

Topher took his wallet from a back pocket and flashed his driver's license.

"Okay." Then the man pointed sternly at Corey. "How 'bout you, miss?"

Corey's stomach fluttered in panic. No ID.

Cutting school. Would the man arrest her?

"She's okay," Topher said. He jerked a thumb at Corey. "Just my kid sister."

Kid sister! Corey opened her mouth to argue when she felt an elbow jab into her ribs. A soft *Ahh* escaped her lips. The guard waved them through the check point.

When they were safely past, Corey tugged roughly at Topher's shirt. "Hey," she said. "What's the idea?"

Topher pulled the cycle off the road, letting the engine idle.

"Gimme a break," he said. "I know that was the worst possible insult, but you wanted to get into the canyon, didn't you?"

Corey glared at him, but said nothing.

"Look," he continued, "I'm not exactly thrilled about that guard thinking you're my sister, but we didn't have a choice. The guards are afraid of looters, and they wouldn't have let you in without ID. So you can owe me an insult, okay?"

"With pleasure," Corey said.

They continued up the road another mile. Corey closed her eyes when they rounded the final bend before her house. She was afraid again. This time, afraid of what she'd see.

The motorcycle made a *blat-blat* sound as the engine stopped.

"We're here," Topher said.

Corey opened her eyes and gasped. She felt as if someone had kicked her in the stomach.

The landscape surrounding her was a sketch done in charcoal. Hills slashed down into the canyon in streaks of gray. Burned trees scratched at the sky with twisted witch fingers. Corey looked up at the blackened chimney that rose ominously above her; at its base lay mangled bits of metal buried in a mound of ash that still smoldered in faint wisps.

"My house," Corey whispered. She moved toward it slowly, as if pushing through water. The sharp bite of smoke filled her nostrils. "It's like that scene in *The Wizard of Oz*." She stared at the rubble in half wonder, half horror. "Dorothy steps from her gray house into that enchanted land of color. Colors so bright they hurt your eyes. This is like that— only in reverse."

Topher interrupted with sarcasm. "Look, Toto. We're back in Kansas."

Corey ignored him. She moved again, cringing when she saw the burned hulk that had been Pete's car. No wonder her brother was upset! Carefully, she picked her way around large, charred beams and sharp pieces of metal, maneuvering past the carcass of a refrigerator, a bathtub. Glass crunched under her feet. Lingering embers warmed the soles of her shoes. She stopped.

What's the matter with me? Corey thought. I should be crying or screaming. She wished she could feel something: the sting of tears in her eyes, the heart-stopping surge of total anger. Pain. Violence. *Anything*.

She waited, trying to absorb what she saw around her, waiting for the impact. Nothing.

"My house," she repeated, as if trying to remind herself. "My *home*."

Topher's jeering voice cut through her thoughts. "Hey, you're not the only one, you know. God, kid, don't you have any feelings?"

Corey's body tingled as if she had been asleep and was slowly awakening. She whirled to face Topher. She hated him more than ever. For chasing Jabber, for his nasty remarks.

"Feelings?" she said. "You're a great one to talk. You're the one who doesn't have any feelings. Why'd you bring me up here, anyway? You get your jollies out of seeing people hurt? In pain? Well, sorry to disappoint you, pal. I won't give you the satisfaction." She trudged through the debris, back to the cycle. "Just leave me alone. Why should I care about you and your house? You don't care about me."

"You got that right," Topher said angrily. He kicked a piece of metal; it tumbled down the hill, clanking against the street below. "I learned long ago not to care about anyone—or anything. When you do, you only put yourself on the line. You get hurt. Trampled. Or ignored."

A truck rumbled by. The bright red call letters of a local television station were painted on the side.

"It's like them." Topher spit out the words. "They don't care. Have you seen the news stories about the fire?" He shoved his fist under Corey's nose. "Tell me, Widow Jones, how does it feel to have your house burn down? Mr. and Mrs. America, kindly tell the folks at home what's it like to lose everything you've worked for? To have your neighborhood turned into a charred wasteland because some stupid kids were playing with matches?" He dropped his hand in resignation. "But they don't ask us. They don't care. We're just kids, so our feelings aren't important. They won't listen. No one will listen—" He turned abruptly. "Doesn't matter, anyway. They wouldn't understand."

Corey heard a small, aching part of herself in his words. Her anger softened to concern.

"Topher," she said quietly. "I—I'll listen. I know how you feel. I understand."

"No. You can't."

"Topher—"

He seemed to look through her now, as if talking to himself. "How can you understand? You've lived here forever. Took it all for granted." He sighed. "Well, not me. I waited six years to have a real home like you had. That was the problem, I guess. Same old story. I cared too much, and look what happened." He swept his hand before them. "Do you know what it's like to care too much? To love a house and love it so bad you can't think of ever leaving it? To wake up in the morning and smile because you feel safe and secure and—" His voice fell to a whisper. "—and happier than you've ever thought possible?"

Why, he's like me, Corey thought. Aloud she said, "I've always felt like that about this place." Her voice caught. "Before—before the fire, I used to wish I had a special camera, so I could frame the canyon in the lens and click!—the shutter would freeze things, stop them from ever changing."

Topher stared at her for a moment. Then his blue, unwavering eyes seemed to cloud over and he turned away again. His shoulders trembled and he made strange choking sounds. Corey watched him in astonishment.

Topher was crying. Big, bad, arrogant, sarcastic Topher was really crying. How she had longed to see him hurt: punished for chasing Jabber and always making her feel like a fool. But not anymore. This—this she couldn't stand. She couldn't bear it.

Tentatively, Corey put her hand on his shoulder. She had never held a guy before, a guy who wasn't her father or Pete. But suddenly she had her arms around Topher. She liked the feeling of his strong arms as he clung to her. She liked the faint shampoo smell of his hair that tickled her neck.

She held him for a long time, trying to show him with her comforting arms how much she understood. But it wasn't enough. She sensed that his tears were caused by a pain much deeper than the loss of his home.

A pain she had no right to ask about.

After a while, Topher pulled away. He wiped his eyes with the back of his hand and headed back to the motorcycle.

Corey started after him. "Topher—"

He stopped, but didn't turn around. "I'd like to be alone for a while," he said. "Why don't you go look for your cat."

"Oh. Okay." Corey watched him walk away. The old Topher was back. The few moments of openness, tenderness, were gone.

She moved to the edge of her property and stood motionless, looking down into the canyon. The foothills were dotted with dozens of smoldering ruins that had once been fine homes. Could Jabberwocky still be alive somewhere in that desolation? Everything looked dead. Destroyed. Everything, except—

There. She could see one house. It sat perfect and whole. The sun glimmered and glistened on its roof, reflected like diamonds in the windows.

Ericka's house.

Corey swallowed against the ice cube, cold and aching in her throat. She closed her eyes, unable to bear the scene.

If only things could be like they were before. If only . . .

Her body swayed. She opened her eyes and sighed. Then she set off to search for Jabberwocky.

CHAPTER
10

"MISS JOHNSON, do you have an excuse for yesterday's absence?" Mr. Yenke's voice boomed gruffly across the classroom, his thick gray eyebrows furled with impatience.

Hearing her name, Corey automatically turned her gaze away from the door where she had been watching for Topher. She gave the algebra teacher a bewildered look. An excuse?

Her heart stopped cold.

An excuse. She had forgotten about cutting classes yesterday afternoon. None of the other teachers had mentioned her absence. In light of the fire, they probably thought it unnecessary to question her.

But oh, no, Corey thought. Not Mr. Yenke. He was the strictest teacher at Santa Barbara High. If she had a heart attack right now, right here, he'd refuse to give her a hall pass to get into the ambulance.

"Well?" Mr. Yenke demanded.

"Well—" Corey echoed. Several kids snickered. "Well, there was a fire last weekend and my—"

Mr. Yenke interrupted her with an impatient gesture. "Yes, Miss Johnson, I know about the fire. But did you get an absence card from the main office?"

"Um. No, but—"

"I see." The teacher marked something in his attendance book. "Ladies and gentlemen, please take out last night's homework. Miss Johnson, five demerits."

Corey heard the guy behind her give a low whistle. Her cheeks flamed. Five demerits. That would ruin her citizenship record.

Big deal, she told herself angrily. Things like demerits and algebra weren't important compared to what she had seen yesterday.

She forgot Mr. Yenke's angry eyebrows as she glanced at Topher's empty desk by the window.

Where was he? Had he cut class again to go up to the canyon? Or because he couldn't face her? Topher hadn't spoken one word to her the rest of the afternoon until they returned to the school parking lot.

"See you," he said coldly, his face averted, hidden behind disheveled curls. Then he roared away, leaving Corey to sit alone on the curb, waiting for her mother, sorting out painful images of the afternoon.

It had all been so unreal. Finding her home

in smoldering ruins. Her jumbled thoughts at seeing Ericka's house whole, Ericka's world safe and unchanged. And Topher—speaking of secret feelings she thought were only her own, and then—his tears.

Corey shook her head. Worse than all that, she had spent over two hours in the canyon without finding Jabberwocky.

She hadn't told her parents about the canyon trip with Topher, knowing both of them would disapprove. But at breakfast that morning, she again brought up the subject of Jabber, hoping they would finally realize how much she missed the cat and take her to look for him.

"No, not today," her father said. "This is my first day back at the office and I have lots of patients." Seeing the scowl on Corey's face, he continued sternly, "And don't get any ideas about going up to the canyon alone. Even with the National Guard, there have been problems with looters. It's dangerous to be up there alone. Who knows what could happen to you?"

Mrs. Johnson echoed her husband. "Dad's right, Corey. I wish you wouldn't get your hopes up. From what I've read about the fire, I—" A short pause. "I don't think there's much chance of finding Jab."

Corey didn't believe her. It wasn't true. Jabberwocky was alive up there somewhere and she'd find him. So what if her parents wouldn't help? She had her own plan.

After school, Corey rode downtown with her mother.

"I hope you don't mind," Mrs. Johnson said. "I need to pick up a few odds and ends at Thrifty's." She nosed the compact car into a parking space. "There are so many things we use every day that we don't think about, until they're gone. Like cotton balls and alarm clocks and emery boards." Her voice sounded tired. "Want to come in? Anything you need?"

"No, I'll just wait in the car, Mom. Don't hurry." Corey waited until her mother disappeared into the store, then walked two blocks to the *Daily News* building.

A bored-looking woman with pink, dangling earrings stood behind the counter of the Want Ads section.

"May I help you?" she asked. She sounded as if she didn't care to help Corey at all.

"I'd like to place an ad in the Lost and Found, please."

The woman handed Corey a form and a pen. "Fill this out. Bring it back to me." She spoke in a rehearsed voice. "Then see the cashier."

"Thank you." Corey nibbled thoughtfully on the end of the pen. She caught the woman glaring at the instrument. It was a *Daily News* pen. Hastily, Corey took it out of her mouth. "Sorry," she said. On the form she wrote: *Lost: Black cat, male. Ten years old. Answers to Jabberwocky. Last seen the night of the fire in Sycamore Canyon area. If found, call Corey Johnson, Playa Azul Motel, room 224.*

Corey reread the paragraph. Not bad, but it needed something more. At the bottom of the paper she wrote *Reward*. She had saved almost fifty dollars of her babysitting money. She needed the money to buy Christmas presents for her family, but they'd understand.

Corey returned the form to the woman, who skimmed it for errors.

"Okay, looks fine. If we run this one week, that'll come to thirty-two dollars." The woman jerked her head toward the cashier's window, her earrings jangling noisily. "Pay over there."

Corey didn't move. Thirty-two dollars! That was over half her money. Well, it was worth the whole fifty if it helped her find Jab.

She reached for her purse, then stopped.

She didn't have a purse.

She didn't have any money.

Everything she had, had burned.

"Oh," Corey said softly. Her face flushed.

"What's the matter?" the woman asked warily.

"Um—I guess I left my money at—at home. Can you bill me?"

"Sorry." The woman tore the ad in two. "Against our policy. Come back when you have the cash."

Corey raced back to the car, frustrated. Her mother was waiting for her.

"Where have you been?" Mrs. Johnson asked. "I was starting to worry."

Briefly, Corey explained about the ad. "Mom, could you loan me the money? I promise I'll pay you back as soon as I can."

"Honey, I told you before, we have to watch our finances carefully right now. We can only afford to buy things we really need."

Corey swelled with anger. "Like alarm clocks and—and nail files?"

Her mother frowned. "I don't appreciate that tone."

"Mom, Jabberwocky is something I really need. I can go without clothes for a while and use that money for the ad."

Her mother sighed and started the car. "Honey, please don't hassle me about this. Try to understand. We don't have the cash right now. We're not sure when the insurance money will come through, and we'll need every penny in our bank account for the new house. Besides, it's impractical to spend money on an ad when Jabber is probably—" She bit her lip. "I know—why not try advertising in the school paper? It's free. By the end of next week, we should have some money from the insurance company. If you haven't heard anything about Jabber by then, I'll place an ad for you in the *Daily*. All right?"

"A week!" Corey cried. "Mom, Jabber could starve by then. He could *die*."

"Corey, I know you loved that cat. We all

did. But I think you have to face the fact that he's already dead."

A strained silence.

"Corey?"

Corey said nothing. She stared out the window, her jaw set in a firm line. There seemed little point in arguing with her mother. Jabber was alive and she had to find him. Why couldn't anyone understand that?

Back at the motel, Mrs. Johnson noticed a red light lit on their phone. "We have a message," she said, dialing the front office. She spoke to the desk clerk, then replaced the receiver. "It's for you, Corey. Ericka phoned. You're supposed to call her back."

Probably wondering where I've been, Corey thought. She had avoided Ericka that day by eating lunch in an isolated part of the school. For some reason, she didn't feel like seeing her friend. And she didn't want to talk to her now.

"Corey, did you hear me? Ericka called. Better call her back."

Corey switched on the television. "I will, as soon as this program is over." But the program ended and another took its place. Corey managed to put off calling Ericka all afternoon. It wasn't until she and her parents returned from dinner that she finally dialed the Smiths' number.

"Corey? Is that you?" Mrs. Smith asked. "Wait a minute. Let me call Ericka." There was the muffled sound of a hand being placed over the receiver. "Ericka? Ericka! Lyn, run tell your sister that Corey's on the phone." The hand was removed and Corey could hear the youngest daughter screeching for Ericka. Television voices murmured in the background. A dishwasher chugged rhythmically. Corey felt a pang of sadness. She missed those sounds. Dumb, ordinary sounds. The sounds of *home*.

"Corey, dear," Mrs. Smith was saying. "We're all so sorry about your house. This has been a nightmare. Is your family all right?"

"Yes," Corey heard herself say. She had to force herself to sound polite. "We're all fine."

"I'm so relieved. Tell your mom to call me if she needs anything, hear me? And if you get tired of the motel, remember, our home is your home."

"Sure. Thanks," Corey said.

Ericka's voice came on the line.

"Corey, where've you been the last two days? I waited for you at lunch."

"I—I've had other things to do," Corey said. She couldn't explain to Ericka about wanting to eat alone, or about not wanting to eat at all. She couldn't tell her about cutting school with Topher, either. Those things seemed too personal to share. And to think she used to tell Ericka everything! "I've been busy since—since the fire," Corey added lamely.

"That's okay. I understand," Ericka said. "But let's get together soon, okay? Maybe later this week. The party's in a week and a half."

Corey's mind went blank. "What party?"

"Corey, do you have amnesia or something? The Halloween party! The King and Queen of Hearts, remember?"

"You mean you're still going to have it?"

"Sure. I know, too soon after the fire, right? But that's exactly why we should have it. Psychologically, it'll be good for us to get involved in something. Take our minds off of—well, you know."

Off what? Corey thought. What did Ericka have to be upset about? Aloud she said, "Oh, I don't know, Ericka. I don't feel much like partying."

"But, Corey, the party won't be any fun without you. Besides, you always come up with the best ideas. Can't you help just a little?" Ericka pleaded. "All we need is one afternoon to get things arranged. Please?"

Corey sighed. "Oh, all right."

"Great, Corey, I knew I could count on you! Want to come over after school on Friday?"

Corey thought of sunshine, glimmering on Ericka's windows. "No! I mean, no, I—I think it'll be better if we meet at school. I'll ask Mom to pick me up at four-thirty."

"Okay," Ericka said. "Let's meet outside in the quad. At three." A pause. "Hey, will I see you tomorrow at lunch?"

"No, I don't think so."

"Oh. Well, okay." Ericka sounded bewildered.

"Guess I'll talk to you on Friday. Thanks, Corey. I'm glad you're gonna help me. You'll see, this will be a great party!"

Corey hung up the phone, feeling an edge of anger inside. She had a sudden desire to hurt Ericka, a desire to yawn and say: *Oh, costume parties are so boring. When are you going to grow up?*

She envisioned the hurt look on Ericka's face. Then Ericka's face turned into her own. Corey suddenly knew, deep down, that she really wanted to go to that party and have a great time. But she had a sinking suspicion that she might never have a great time again.

CHAPTER
11

AFTER SEVENTH PERIOD on Friday, Corey hurried to place her ad about Jabberwocky in the *Forge*, the school newspaper. Wistfulness tugged inside her. If her mother had loaned her money for the *Daily* ad, Jabber might be "home" already. But no amount of pleading had changed Mrs. Johnson's mind. Now it would be more than a week before Corey could expect to hear anything about her cat. The *Forge* accepted classifieds on Fridays only, and the next issue wouldn't be printed until the following Friday—two weeks after Jabber's disappearance. Didn't her mother realize every day counted? Jabberwocky could be hurt. Or dying.

She pushed those thoughts away as she entered the English building. The *Forge* office bustled with activity. Newspapers hadn't been delivered to all the classrooms yet, and students rushed about with intent faces, shouting orders, trying to pass through the door on both sides of her.

A dark-haired girl with glasses, seated at a desk across the room, looked the least busy of anyone. Corey approached her, trying not to slip on scraps of paper that littered the floor.

The girl removed her glasses, revealing wide, dark eyes with thick, black lashes. She smiled. "Need some help?" She spoke with a slight Mexican accent.

Corey handed her a piece of paper from her notebook. "Can you place this ad in your Classifieds for next week?"

The girl slipped on her glasses again. She read the copy, absently twirling a pencil between her fingers.

I should be placing *two* lost and founds, Corey thought. Topher still hadn't shown up at school. Maybe he figured the longer he stayed away from her, the better. Corey dreaded their next meeting. It was doomed to be awkward. And yet something about him kept her waiting to see his face in algebra.

"Oh, wow," the girl said, looking up. "I'm sorry about your cat. Did you lose your house, too?"

Corey gave a stiff nod. She braced herself, prepared for the usual pitying glance most kids had been giving her all week.

"I can sympathize with you," the girl said. "I lost my house in a fire once, too."

"You did?" Corey said, caught by surprise.

"Uh-huh. I was only six, so I don't remember everything. But as Dad tells the story,

Mom was trying to be a real chef in the kitchen and we ended up with House Flambé as our main course." A short laugh. "Mom still isn't a very good cook."

Corey smiled, relaxing a little.

"Pleased to meet you, fellow fire victim," the girl said. "That's what the press has dubbed you, isn't it? My name's Anna Mendoza." She stuck out her hand. "Future Pulitzer Prize winner."

Uncomfortably, Corey took Anna's hand. She'd never shaken hands with anyone near her own age before. "My name's Corey."

"Well, Corey, bad news. We're in financial straits this year, so I'm afraid I'll have to charge you for this ad. However—" Anna paused and tilted her head, looking at Corey with a conspirator's smile. "I have a proposition for you. I'll run your ad for free, if you help me with an important article I have to write."

"Me? I don't know anything about journalism."

"No . . . see, I want to interview you," Anna explained. "Next week, the *Forge* is running a series of articles about the Sycamore Fire. History of similar fires, fire prevention, insurance problems, things like that. I'm supposed to write an article about kids from Santa Barbara High who've lost their homes." A sigh. "Having a heck of a time, too. One family has already moved away. And one kid I approached, a guy in motocross boots, wouldn't say a word. In fact, I thought he was gonna belt me!"

Corey repressed a grin. Topher!

"Anyway, would you mind if I interviewed you?"

"Well, I don't know," Corey began.

"Look, I promise you can read the article before it goes to press. And if there's anything you don't like, well—" Anna made an erasing motion in the air with her pencil. "—out it goes. No problem, okay?"

Corey swallowed uncomfortably. She'd be the feature of this article, and everyone at school would read about her and her problems. She wasn't sure she liked that idea.

Chicken Little rides again! Here was a chance to get a free ad about Jabber, and she was hedging just because she was afraid of what the other kids would think or say.

"Okay," Corey said, a spark of determination flaring inside her. "I'll do it."

"All right!" Anna's face broke into a wide smile. "Do you have time for an interview now? My deadline's Wednesday. I could use the weekend to write."

"Sure! My mom isn't picking me up until four-thirty."

"Great." Anna gathered up a few notebooks and a tape recorder. "This place is a zoo. Let's head over to McDonald's. Quieter there. And we can sit at a table outside. I'll buy you a Coke."

The two girls were walking near the edge of campus when Corey heard someone calling her name. She turned to see Ericka, hurrying breathlessly after them.

"Corey, where are you going? I've been waiting for you in the quad for twenty minutes."

Corey looked blankly at her friend for a few seconds. Then she remembered. "Oh, Ericka, the Halloween party! I'm sorry! I forgot I was gonna meet you. Hey, meet Anna Mendoza. She works on the *Forge* and wants to interview me about the fire."

Ericka smiled in Anna's direction. "Hi. That's great, Corey. But what about the party? We've got to finish planning. Can't you do the interview another time?"

"We'll, I've got a deadline to meet," Anna said. "But if you already had plans, Corey, we—"

"Ericka, this is really important," Corey broke in. "I'll call you tomorrow, okay? We'll get together then."

A pause.

"Okay, Ericka?"

"Okay, sure, whatever you say." Ericka's voice was breezy. She shrugged. "I certainly don't want to stand in the way of your publicity." She wheeled around and started to walk away.

Corey felt a twinge of guilt—and relief. She'd been dreading this meeting with Ericka since Tuesday night. Now the meeting was postponed, perhaps indefinitely.

"I'll phone you tomorrow, Ericka," Corey called after her. "Really. I promise."

Ericka gave a curt wave without looking back.

Corey fell into step again with Anna, trying to shake off the lingering feeling of guilt. She had plainly seen that her decision hurt Ericka. Well, she'd get over it in time. That's what friends were for, wasn't it?

A few minutes later, Corey and Anna sat at a picnic table under a bright orange umbrella. It felt cool in the shade, and Corey pulled on her once-hated-now-loved pink sweater. Fall had finally arrived. Funny. In some ways, Corey felt as if she were surrounded by the bleakest of winters.

"Don't let this bother you," Anna said as she fiddled with the tape recorder. "It's just to aid my feeble memory." She smiled. "I want this interview to be as informal as possible. More like a conversation. Ready?"

Corey sipped nervously at her Coke. "Ready."

Anna pressed the record button. "Okay, maybe you can start by telling me what you were doing the night of the fire."

Corey thought back to that night. Waiting for Topher . . . sirens wailing . . . dark columns of smoke. "I—I was at home," she answered vaguely.

"Alone?"

"Well, no. I had a—a friend with me."

Strange. Topher had once been her worst enemy.

"Yes?" Anna prompted.

"Anna," Corey began, "do you mind if we don't talk about that night? It—it's kind of personal."

"Okay, we'll go on to something else. Did you lose everything in the fire? What do you miss the most?"

Corey was silent for a moment. Then she began to talk. About Jabberwocky. And Pete's silences. And the house she loved so much. Anna made only a few comments, but she looked up at Corey now and then. The expression on her face made Corey feel as if Anna were holding her hand—not in sympathy, but in total understanding. And of course, Anna would understand. After all, her house had once burned down, too.

When the tape ejected automatically from the recorder, Corey jumped, surprised. She had been talking about the fire for forty-five minutes!

"It's almost four-thirty," Anna said. "Just a couple more questions." She flipped the tape to the other side. "What's your overall feeling about what's happened to you?"

Corey glanced up at the blackened foothills. "I felt sort of numb, at first. And the first day, back at school, I couldn't understand how the other kids could just laugh and act naturally. I mean, I felt like a stone thrown into a pond.

100

And the ripples of what had happened should have spread out to the other kids . . ."

"And now?" Anna asked.

"Now, I'm scared," Corey continued. "My life has changed so much. And I hate that. I feel as if everything and everyone I've ever loved has been taken away. I feel empty . . . and alone."

Anna nodded. She was silent for a few moments. "So what's next for you and your family? Do you think you'll rebuild?"

Rebuild. Corey hadn't thought of that before. She'd bitten her nails, worrying about moving away or remaining at the motel or other horrible alternatives. How stupid! Of course they'd rebuild. With the insurance money, they could hire a contractor and be home by— why, maybe by spring!

"Oh, yes," Corey said with new confidence. "Yes, we're going to rebuild." Oh, it had to be true. Hadn't her mother said they needed all their money for the new house? Hadn't she overheard her talking to Dad about furniture and dishes? She hadn't paid much attention to the conversations, but now . . .

Her heart gave a little hop. They were going to rebuild. Life would soon be exactly as it was before!

"You did great, Corey," Anna was saying. "Thanks. I'll write the article this weekend and let you read it Tuesday afternoon. We'll get together for Cokes again, okay?"

"Okay!" Corey barely heard her. She was so excited, she pumped Anna's hand, then practically ran all the way to the school parking lot.

"You seem awfully happy this afternoon," her mother said, as Corey got in the car. "Something good happen at school?"

Quickly, Corey told her mother about the interview and the ad.

"That's wonderful, sweetheart," Mrs. Johnson said. "And I have just the thing to put the icing on your cake." She turned right on State Street and drove uptown, away from the beach.

"What do you mean?" Corey asked. "And where are we going?"

Mrs. Johnson gave her daughter a sly smile. "No questions. You'll just have to be surprised." She hummed softly.

"Okay, be that way," Corey said with a laugh. She adjusted her seat belt and settled back to enjoy the ride. It felt good to have Mom acting like herself again.

After a few miles, they turned off the main street into a quiet suburb. Here the houses were old and quaint, most of them built in the early nineteen-thirties. The car turned into the driveway of a cream-colored house with brown trim and shutters. Corey thought the house looked like something out of *Hansel and Gretel*.

"Who lives here?" she asked her mother.

Mrs. Johnson smiled happily. "We do."

CHAPTER
12

"ARE YOU SERIOUS?" Corey asked. She followed her mother up an old flagstone walkway to the front door of the house. "This is really ours?"

"We rented it yesterday," Mrs. Johnson said. "Dad and I didn't want to tell you right away. Without furniture, we weren't sure when we could move in." She unlocked the door with a large brass key. "As it turned out, we had a stroke of good luck."

Corey stepped over the threshold. Her shoes clunked loudly on a golden hardwood floor.

"Where'd this stuff come from?" she asked. The living room held a faded couch, two scuffed straightback chairs and a small coffee table. A bright red painting, tilted on its side, hung above the stone fireplace. Corey thought it looked like a picture of a Hawaiian shirt.

Her mother laughed, the sound echoing in the half-empty house. "Quite a mishmash of stuff, isn't it? When the landlord heard about our situation, he cleaned out his garage. This furniture is on loan until we buy our own. Or until these fall apart, whichever comes first."

Corey smiled wryly. "If this is the good luck, I'd hate to see the bad."

"We've already had that." Her mother's tone was resentful. Then her good spirits returned. "Come on, I'll give you the Grand Tour."

The tour didn't take long. There was a living room, a small dining room, a kitchen, a tiny bath, and two bedrooms.

"This will be your room," Mrs. Johnson said. "Needs a quick paint job. We'll have to get you some drapes, too, but at least you'll get plenty of sunshine in the mornings."

Corey peeked in to the room and caught a faint whiff of mothballs.

"I hung up your clothes in the closet," her mother continued. "Sorry, the landlord didn't have a bed for you, just that sleeping bag. Pretend you're a Girl Scout again."

"Where's Pete going to sleep?" Corey asked.

"He can use the couch in the living room until we get a hide-a-bed. Being at school most of the year, he won't need a room of his own." Mrs. Johnson whirled suddenly like a child. "It feels so good to be out of that motel! I knew we couldn't get our lives back to normal again until we found a home. So what do you think?"

"It's a cute house," Corey said. "I like it." The house was old, but clean and well cared-for. It would be a nice place to stay until their own home was rebuilt.

"Oh, look at the time." Mrs. Johnson hurried down the hall, calling back over her shoulder,

"I've got to get my roast in the oven. I borrowed a few pots and dishes and some silverware from Ericka's mom. We're going to have a real dinner celebration tonight."

Corey moved to help her mother.

"No, it's okay," Mrs. Johnson said. Then, in her best John Wayne imitation, she added, "The kitchen ain't big enough for the both of us." She smiled. "Why don't you set the table, then explore the neighborhood? There's an old bike in the garage. Another loaner from the landlord."

"Great." Corey set three plates on the wobbly card table in the dining room. Then she grabbed her new jacket and hastened to the garage, eager for a ten-speed cruise in the fall air.

She was instantly disappointed. The bike lay on its side next to a pile of rags. Corey lifted it, warily eyeing its ramshackle appearance. Rust freckled the body and cobwebs tangled the spokes. The seat tilted at a precarious angle.

"This thing should be dead and buried," Corey muttered, mourning for her own bike. She dusted it off as best she could with an old rag. Then she wheeled it out to the driveway.

With a strong push, she was riding through the evening, past rows of fairy-tale homes with tiny, manicured lawns. Windows glowed friendly and yellow-warm in the twilight. Corey felt almost happy. She had thought Mom and Dad had let her down, but all along they'd been making plans to take care of her, just as always. And soon, very soon, they'd be home again in the canyon.

She took a deep breath. The neighborhood smelled of crisp leaves and the mingling aromas of dinner. Suddenly, for the first time in a week, Corey was ravenous. She pedaled home swiftly, brakes squealing in front of the house. She hoped dinner would be ready soon.

"This is wonderful," Dr. Johnson said two hours later, when they sat down to dinner. A candle burned cozily on the table. Mrs. Johnson poured him a glass of wine. "A toast—to our new home." He and his wife clinked glasses then saluted Corey and her milk.

"You know," Dr. Johnson continued, "I think I'll like living here. Took the bus from town, and it stops right down at the corner. I walked the last four blocks home. Couldn't have planned it any better." He took the platter his wife handed him and selected a large slice of rare meat. "So, Smiley," he said to Corey. "How do you like the new abode?"

Corey held up a finger. She had just filled her mouth with mashed potatoes and rich gravy. She chewed blissfully. "It's delicious," she answered, eyes half-closed.

Her father chuckled.

"Oh, you mean the house." Corey giggled. "It's cute. That picture in the living room has to go, but the rest of the house is fine. It'll be nice living here for a while."

"Aren't you rushing things a bit?" Dr. Johnson asked. "College is still four years away for you."

"No, I mean the house is fine till we rebuild our old one."

Her parents exchanged glances. "I don't think you understand, Corey," her father said. He gestured with his fork. "*This* is going to be our home. For good. We signed a year's lease with an option to buy."

Corey felt cold. Her words came slow and even. "I—don't—understand."

"We decided it was time for a smaller house," Dr. Johnson explained. "Our old one was beautiful, but so large and expensive to heat. We'd planned to sell it eventually, after you graduated from college. The fire sped our plans up a bit. We don't intend to rebuild."

With a deliberate effort, Corey placed her fork on the plate. Her stomach felt tight. "What is this 'we' stuff? Nobody consulted *me* about it."

"We thought you'd be pleased," Mrs. Johnson said. "You've been moping about the last week in that motel. Here you have your own room. And, although the school bus doesn't come out to this district, we made sure you can continue at Santa Barbara High. You'll still be with all your friends."

Corey stared at her mother. Her face felt hot with frustration. "But, Mom, I thought we were supposed to work together now, make decisions as a family. Nobody asked me if I wanted to live here. It wasn't a family decision. Does Pete know?"

"No. Not yet."

"I don't believe it," Corey whispered.

"Honey, why are you so upset?" her mother asked. "We really thought you'd be pleased. We even planned to get you a kitten at the Humane Society. Now that Jabber is gone, a new cat might—"

"No!" Corey put her hands over her ears. "I won't listen to you. Jabber isn't dead. He isn't! Did you think you could bribe me, like you did when I was five? Well, I'm not five anymore. I'm fourteen. Don't you care how I feel? Don't my opinions count? I hate this house. I don't want to live here. I want to go home!"

She threw down her napkin and ran to her room, slamming the door.

But what good did it do, running here, she thought helplessly. She hated this room. At home, her room had been a special place, a comforting place where she could curl up and be alone to resolve her thoughts and problems. This room wasn't a sanctuary. It was a prison. She had nowhere to run anymore.

Corey took off her shoes and climbed into the sleeping bag. She tucked her head to her knees, fists clenched.

Then she knew. Pete. Her big brother, her protector. As soon as Mom and Dad were asleep, she'd call him. He would know what to do, what things to say to make their parents understand.

Corey burrowed deeper into her cocoon, waiting, for what seemed like hours, until the house was quiet. Then she climbed out of the sleeping bag and quietly opened the door to her room. She tiptoed into the hall, and brought the phone on its long cord back to her room. Nervously, she punched Pete's number, hoping he wasn't still mad at her.

The phone rang eight times, then came a sleepy "Hello?"

"Pete?"

"Mmmm. Yeah."

"Pete, it's Corey." Silence. She could hear her heart beating. "Corey, your sister."

"Can't be," his muffled voice answered. "No sister of mine would call me after one in the morning."

Corey felt a flood of relief. He didn't hate her! He was making stupid jokes, so everything had to be okay!

"Pete. Pete, I need to talk to you. I—"

"Okay, okay, Sis," Pete drawled. "Slow down. What's going? First Mom and Dad call me, now you. Is this a conspiracy? I swear, I'm just sleeping. There are no girls in my room."

Corey rushed on. "Mom and Dad called you? Tonight?"

"Yeah. Told me about the house. Dad said you freaked."

"They're the ones who've freaked," Corey lashed out angrily. Then her voice grew soft. "Pete, things are so strange here. Mom still refuses to go up to the canyon, and sometimes she breaks down and cries for no reason. It's scary.

I mean, she's always been so happy, so in control. And Dad, he makes lists and lists of things to do, but nothing ever gets done. He won't even listen to me about Jabber. And now they want to buy this awful house." Corey's voice grew hoarse with emotion. She swallowed against the tightening in her throat. "Pete, you've got to help me. Together we can change their minds. I know if they rebuild, things can be the way they were before. Before everything—changed."

"I don't think so, Sis."

Corey choked back a sob.

"Listen, Corey," Pete continued. He spoke quietly, seriously. "I acted like a real jerk last weekend. I blamed Mom and Dad and especially you for what happened to my car. And the house." A deep breath. "I'm really sorry for the things I said. But see, I hurt. I'm still hurting, just like you. I loved that house and the memories, but I've realized life goes on. And my own life is here, at school."

"Pete, no. Listen—"

"No, you listen, Sis. What I'm trying to say is, it's time for you and Mom and Dad to make a new life. If this new house makes them happy, we can't fight it. It wouldn't be fair. Not after what they've gone through."

"But they won't be happy," Corey wailed miserably. "They're bailing out. And what about me? I feel like a crooked puzzle piece. Where do I fit, Pete?"

"I don't know what to say, Corey. You'll have

to find that out for yourself."

Corey said nothing. She twisted the phone cord around a finger.

"Corey? Are you still there? Listen, call me again if you want. You know I'm always willing to help—"

"Forget it," Corey said, cutting him off. "There's only one way you can help, and you won't do it. Thanks. Thanks a whole lot."

She slammed down the receiver.

Instantly, she regretted her action. She picked up the phone again and punched Pete's number, ready to apologize. No answer. Her brother must have disconnected the phone to finally get some sleep.

Okay, now what? Corey limply weighed the phone in her hand. No one cared. No one understood. So what was the point of staying here, in a place she hated, if she had nothing left?

With a sob of loneliness, she curled back into the sleeping bag. She'd run away. That's what she'd do. No one would care. No one except—Jabberwocky.

She couldn't leave. Not yet, not while he was still missing. Jabber was alive somewhere and she had to find him. She'd go up to the canyon tomorrow, alone, and search again. And when she found him . . .

Corey twisted around in her sleeping bag and closed her eyes. Go to sleep, she told herself. She'd worry about leaving tomorrow—after she found Jabber.

CHAPTER
13

COREY AWAKENED in a pool of sunshine. She sat up, stiff from sleeping on the hard floor, and stared at the large oleander bush outside. Its green leaves, spotted with sun, scratched softly against the windowpane in the autumn breeze. She heard other sounds, too: morning sounds she wasn't used to. Squeaky baby-stroller wheels. The clang of garbage cans. A police siren with dogs singing in harmony. These were city sounds, and Corey hated them. She turned her back to the window.

"Corey? Honey, are you awake?"

Corey heard her mother's soft voice at the bedroom door. She kept silent.

"Corey?"

Go away, Corey thought. She closed her eyes tightly. I'm asleep, go away. She didn't want to see her mother, didn't want to believe the concern and warmth she heard in her mother's voice. The mom who understood wasn't there anymore. That mom had been lost in the fire.

After a moment, Mrs. Johnson's steps receded down the hall. Voices murmured and the front door closed. Corey was alone.

She crawled out of the sleeping bag, noticing she still wore her school clothes. She changed into jeans and a pale green sweater. In the kitchen she found a note taped to the refrigerator.

Corey: Breakfast goodies inside. Dad and I've gone shopping. Back later this afternoon. Love you, Mom.

Corey felt ashamed. Her mother hadn't mentioned last night's outburst, and there was a large heart drawn around the word *Love*.

Mom was still Mom, Corey thought, Somewhere, deep inside, Mom was there. But could she ever reach that person again?

Corey ran to the garage and wheeled out the old bicycle. She remembered her dad's words, warning her about going to the canyon alone, but she didn't care. Nothing would happen to her. Nothing mattered except Jabberwocky.

An hour later, Corey reached the ruins of her home. She dropped the bike in disgust, then collapsed beside it, exhausted.

"You—are—" she told it breathlessly, "a—piece—of—junk!" The bicycle chain had fallen off four times during the long, slow ride up the canyon road. Corey wiped a thread of sweat from her forehead with a greasy hand. At least the ride back would be mostly downhill.

She relaxed against a burned tree trunk and surveyed the canyon. Peaceful as always. Maybe too peaceful. Corey thought the air should be alive with wild, bursting sounds.

The heavy silence seemed incongruous with the violence of the landscape.

Loud footsteps broke the silence. Someone was coming up the driveway. Who could it be? The National Guard had been recalled yesterday. There was no one to protect her. Her father's words flashed through Corey's mind: . . . *dangerous to be up there alone* . . . A chill snaked down her back.

The footsteps grew louder. He was right behind her! Corey's hand shot out, groping in the ash for something, anything, to use as protection. Then she was on her feet, a long, hard object held high above her head.

Topher's blue eyes widened in astonishment when he saw the metal pipe in her hand.

"Oh, it's you," Corey said. She dropped the pipe in relief. "I'm sorry. I—I thought you were a looter."

"Sure," Topher said, "burned merchandise has a great resale value."

A blush crept into Corey's cheeks. "Pretty dumb, huh? I should've known better. You startled me, that's all." She glanced at her shoes, bracing herself. Here it comes. He'd zing her good this time.

"I'm glad you came today," Topher said.

Corey looked up in surprise. This was not the sarcastic remark she'd expected. "You—what?"

"I'm glad you're here." Topher's words came slowly, as if he were choosing them with care.

114

"I wanted to apologize. For Monday. I was pretty upset and—"

"It's okay," Corey broke in hurriedly. "I understand. You don't have to explain. Unless of course you want to." She was flustered now. "I mean, if you want to talk about it, that's okay. If not, that's okay, too."

"Thanks." Topher's mouth turned up slightly at the corners. It was the first time Corey had seen him smile.

Self-consciously, she moved her foot in tiny toe circles in the ash.

A moment passed.

"So what are you doing up here?" Topher asked. He seemed anxious to change the subject.

"Jabberwocky, my cat, is still missing. I thought I'd look around for him again. And I—" She paused. "I wanted to get away. We're not living at the motel anymore. My parents rented a house. They want to buy it."

"I'm sorry," Topher said.

Corey couldn't help smiling. "If you were a normal person, you would've said you were glad."

"I'm not normal." Topher's voice held a serious note. Then he flashed his crooked smile. "Besides, I want to move back here, just like you. That's why I'm here now. Come on. I'll show you what I've done this week."

Corey followed him across the charred field to his property. She gasped in surprise. The cement foundation of his house was almost completely clear of debris. Ash and rubble stood in neat, separate piles in the driveway.

"You did all this yourself?" she asked.

"Yeah. I borrowed a shovel and wheelbarrow from the high school. The work wasn't hard. But I need some help moving the bigger stuff. The refrigerator weighs a ton. And it's sharp."

Corey noticed the cuts on Topher's hands. His T-shirt and jeans were coated with a week's worth of ash. No wonder he hadn't been at school! "Why are you doing this?" she asked.

Topher shrugged. "Our house wasn't fully insured. If we spend a lot of money on little things, like renting a bulldozer to clear this stuff away, we may not have enough money to build another home." He looked at Corey, his eyes blue and intense. "And I want another home."

"Me, too," Corey whispered. Oh, if only her parents understood the way Topher did!

"Look at this." Topher sounded like a proud child. He led her down the hill, below where his house had stood. "I had the city reconnect the water main and I planted grass here. I've been watering it every day. The new grass will keep the hill from sliding in the first rains. There's no way we can afford to prop up the hill if it starts to go."

He looked down into the canyon, the breeze touching and lifting his wild curls. "You know, even burned this place is beautiful. Serene. It's hard to work. Sometimes all I want to do is sit and watch the day go by. But I've done enough of that." He sighed. "I've been doing a

116

lot of thinking since Monday. It's time to make some changes. Here—and inside me."

Changes, changes! Corey thought. Everyone wanted to make changes, except her. "Haven't you had enough changes already?" she asked bitterly. She spun away.

"Hey, where're you going?"

"To look for my cat."

"Oh." Corey heard disappointment in Topher's voice. "I don't like cats much."

"I've noticed."

"Yeah, well—" A shadow passed over Topher's face. "You shouldn't be wandering around up here alone. I'll help you look for a while."

"Okay." Corey tried to keep her voice as casual as his. She couldn't believe he actually wanted to help her. "Okay," she repeated, "but then you have to let me help you clear more debris."

"It's a deal," Topher said. "Let's go."

They searched for Jabberwocky well into the afternoon. Corey was surprised at how comfortable she felt around Topher. They didn't talk much, but the awkward, embarrassed silence she'd dreaded never hung over them.

She glanced at Topher once. He hardly seemed aware of her presence. He looked intent, his mouth set in a firm line that matched the line of concentration on his forehead. As they walked, burned chaparral crunched loudly under the weight of his motocross boots. Corey like the sound. It made his steps seem strong and purposeful. How different he was from that wild, faceless phantom of one week ago!

They headed back to her property when the wind turned cold.

Corey shivered, putting her hands into the pockets of her jacket. Dark clouds gathered in the distance. Below her, chimneys cast long, lonely shadows in the late afternoon sun. Corey shivered again, a lonely, shadowy feeling settling inside her.

"Why do you like cats so much?" Topher asked, breaking the silence. He didn't conceal the disdain in his voice.

"Oh, I don't know. I've had Jabber forever. He's a part of me." Corey turned Topher's question over in her mind. "Actually, I like cats 'cause they're so independent. You know, they can hunt for food, keep themselves clean, even play games on their own. Now with dogs, you have to do *everything* for them. All they can do is bark and pant."

"I *like* dogs," Topher said with a slight smile.

Corey laughed. "Oh, well, in *that* case, some dogs are nice. I guess what I'm saying is, it's great to be taken care of. But sometimes I wish I were more like cats. More independent, you know?"

"You're more independent than you think," Topher said quietly. "And really—brave." Then, as if he'd said too much, his tone changed abruptly. "Well, see ya around. I've got more important things to do than look for your independent cat."

The words stung Corey, mingling with the rush of unexpected pleasure she'd felt at being called brave. She followed Topher back down the road, bewildered. Was he going back to his old ways of slinging insults?

"Hey, wait a minute," she called. "You said I could help you clear debris."

"Maybe tomorrow," Topher answered. "It's getting late."

"Well, okay. If you're sure." They had reached the driveway. Corey picked up her bike with a soft groan.

"Great wheels," Topher said sarcastically.

A small ember flared inside Corey. She was about to lash out, when she saw the pain in his eyes. Why was Topher nice one minute and rude the next? Maybe he was as unsure about himself as she was?

Corey's anger faded. She shrugged, then forced a sugary-sweet smile. "Thanks for your help, Topher. I'm glad to see that being a jerk is only your part-time job."

Topher's blue eyes narrowed a bit, as if he were taking a mental step backward. Then he laughed appreciatively.

Bingo! Corey thought.

They stood there, grinning at one another. Suddenly, Corey wanted to say something more. She couldn't let him walk away. Not without letting him know she understood at least a part of him now.

Before she realized what she was saying, she blurted out, "Topher, would you like to go to a Halloween party with me next Friday night?"

Topher looked at her curiously. Corey almost fainted from shock. Now why had she said *that*? Hadn't she learned from the last time? Despite the fire, despite his brief show of emotion, he was still cold, sarcastic Topher. Now it was his cue to say, *Don't do me any favors, kid.*

"I don't have a costume," Topher said.

Corey almost laughed in relief. That remark seemed so absurd at this point. "Me neither. But I'm sure we could rig up something."

Topher hesitated. "I don't know. I'm not big on parties. They can be a real drag."

"I know, but I have to go. Ericka Smith and I have been planning this party since summer."

"I'll think about it and let you know."

"Okay. See you." Corey got on the old bike, her legs feeling wobbly. She'd just asked a guy on a date! And Topher, at that. Maybe she really *was* brave—at least a little more courageous than before. She had to admit, it was a nice change.

Corey started to coast down the driveway. She had gone several yards when she heard Topher calling after her.

"Hey!" he shouted. "I'm sorry I chased your cat!"

Corey turned and waved, then pedaled swifty, a smile forming on her lips. He had finally apologized. And without her father's prodding. That had taken a lot of courage.

A small, warm feeling filled her stomach. In that instant, Corey decided she liked Topher West very much.

CHAPTER
14

COREY REACHED THE NEW HOME at the same time as her parents. The minute she saw them, the warm, pleasant feeling in her stomach vanished. These were strangers. Strangers who didn't understand how lonely she felt, especially without Jabber. She didn't want to talk to them.

"Hi, sweetheart," her father called. He and her mother got out of the car, their arms laden with packages.

"Wait till you see what we bought," Mrs. Johnson said. She unlocked the front door. "New dishes, silverware, winter clothes. And we ordered a new bed for you."

"Oh," Corey said.

"Come see," her mother urged.

"No, thanks. I'm starving," Corey lied. "Have to eat first." She hurried to the kitchen and peered into the refrigerator. Suddenly, her words were true. Her head felt light and dizzy and her stomach grumbled with hunger. Corey realized she hadn't eaten anything since the mashed potatoes at dinner last night. Quickly, she made two pot-roast sandwiches and wolfed them down with a glass of milk.

Her mother came into the kitchen and began unpacking a large box. "Been out for a ride?" she asked.

"Mmmm."

"Where to?"

Corey shrugged.

"Don't you want to see the new dishes?" Mrs. Johnson held up a blue stoneware plate.

Corey ignored the pleading look in her mother's eyes. "Later," she said coolly. "I've got homework." She escaped to her room.

You're acting like a brat, she scolded herself. Giving them the silent treatment, just like when you were a kid.

An hour later, Corey heard her mother calling her for dinner.

"I'm not eating," she answered.

"Why not?"

"I'm not hungry."

"You could at least come out and sit with us. I think we should talk. Corey?"

"I have nothing to say." Corey felt as if she were throwing the words against the door. "You won't listen anyway, so what's the use? You don't care how I feel."

"Honey, that's not true."

"I have nothing to say," Corey repeated.

Mrs. Johnson sighed heavily. "I'm sorry you feel that way."

Me, too, Corey thought. But her parents hadn't given her much choice.

She put on her nightgown and crawled into the sleeping bag. Her muscles ached from the difficult ride to the canyon. She massaged her calves until the motion put her to sleep. She dreamed her mother stood over her saying, *Why are you hurting* me?

Why are you hurting me? Corey shot back. Then she was wrenched out of her sleep, her body soaked in sweat. Someone *was* hurt. She heard a siren and a voice screaming, piercing the night.

Corey leaped up. What had happened? Who screamed? Her heart beat wildly against her chest, propelling her across the room.

"Mom! Dad!" She flung open the bedroom door and raced into the hall, colliding with her father.

"It's all right, Corey," he said. He led her gently back into the bedroom. "Hush, it's all right. Just a police siren. It startled your mom out of a sound sleep. She thought it was another fire. She's fine now." He flicked on the light. "Back to bed, sweetheart. It's cold tonight. Look, you're trembling."

Corey allowed her father to tuck the sleeping bag up close around her. The soft flannel cloth felt warm against ber cheeks, yet she still shivered.

"Dad," she whispered, "why can't we go home? Please take me home."

Dr. Johnson knelt on the worn carpet next to her. "Honey, I can't. Your mom is afraid to see the house—and the canyon she loved—destroyed. I won't force her to go. She'll feel more at ease here, living in the city."

"Oh, sure," Corey said bitterly. "She's really at ease tonight."

"Corey—" Her father's voice held a note of warning.

"I'm sorry, Dad. I didn't mean it to sound that way." Corey raised herself on one elbow. "But if we lived in the canyon, Mom wouldn't have heard that siren at all. Now she'll hear them all the time."

Dr. Johnson smoothed a damp lock of hair from Corey's forehead. "There's nothing I'd like better than going back to the life we had a week ago. But we can't."

Corey wanted to shout, *Why not? The Robles are moving back to the canyon. And the Williamses, too!* But she couldn't let her dad know that she'd seen their old neighbors working on their ruined homes. Couldn't let him know she'd been up to the canyon.

"This is our home now," Dr. Johnson was saying. "It's a good place for your mom and me to retire."

"Retire! Dad, you're only forty-two. And you had so many plans for the house. Adding a studio for Mom. And a swimming pool—"

"Things change, Corey." His expression grew wistful. "Try to understand. Your mother and I bought that land in Sycamore Canyon right after we were first married. I was still in dental school. We scrimped and saved to finally build our dream house. It took us years. And I'm just not sure if we're strong enough to start all over again." A sigh. "See, sometimes when a disaster happens, you have to get as far away from the pain as possible to make life bearable. I guess that's why your mother and I like this house so much. We'll be happy here. And you will, too."

"No." Corey pounded her fist into the folds of the sleeping bag. "I don't want to live here. I hate this house. I'll run away!"

"That's enough, Corey." Dr. Johnson's eyes were piercing. "You're acting like a spoiled child. I want you to listen a minute. Your mother lost two things in the fire that were very dear to her, our home and her photography. Now she feels she's losing you, too. You've been nothing but stubborn and cold and rude the last couple of days and it's torturing her. I won't tolerate it." He took a deep breath. "Starting right now, you're to treat your mother with the love and respect she deserves. And I don't want to hear any more pleading or wailing about moving back to the canyon. Our house is gone. You have to face it. It takes time to heal wounds, I know. But you're not helping by twisting the knife this way. Do you understand?"

Corey said nothing. She picked a piece of lint from the sleeping bag and rolled it between her fingers.

"Do you understand?" Dr. Johnson repeated.

"Yes," Corey said woodenly.

"That's my baby. Thank you." He kissed her on the cheek. "You'll be happy here, you'll see. These things just take time. Good night."

When her father had gone, Corey lay down in the darkness, her throat feeling tight and sore. She swallowed hard.

Our house is gone. You have to face it.

Maybe her dad was right. She had been acting like a spoiled child. But were her parents any more grownup? Mom refusing to see the canyon, Dad moving them away. They were hiding, running from the truth, too.

Our house is gone. You have to face it.

Corey burrowed deeper into the bag. If only she could reach out and find Jabberwocky, curled at her feet. His purring would comfort her. Oh, he couldn't be dead. He was the last link, the only link to the things she loved. Tomorrow, after she helped Topher in the canyon, she'd search for Jabber again.

Corey never got the chance. She awoke the next morning to a muted, clapping sound on the roof. Rain. The city was slick and gray with it. She was trapped inside all day, under the watchful gaze of her father. Corey kept her word to him and acted kinder to her mother.

126

But the warmth she had once felt toward her parents was gone. She didn't belong anymore. She was only a polite guest, living in a house with distant relatives.

The rain continued on Monday, and Corey was relieved to get back to school. But her relief flashed to panic and guilt when she spotted Ericka in the main hall. Rats. She'd forgotten to call her friend about the Halloween party. Despite her reluctance to help plan the festivities, Corey knew she at least owed Ericka an apology.

"Hey, Ericka," she called.

"Oh, hello, stranger," Ericka said coolly. She knotted her pullover sweater around her neck and started to walk away.

"Wait up, Ericka. Listen, I'm really sorry I didn't call you this weekend. We were so busy with our new house and everything, that I just forgot."

Ericka said nothing.

"Do you want to get together this afternoon?"

"No, thanks. I don't need you anymore, Corey. I got Susan Rehler to help me yesterday. The party's all planned."

"Susan *'Airhead'*? Are you crazy? She'll probably decorate your house with Santa Claus pictures. What a space cadet!"

"I think she's nice," Ericka said with an injured air. "The best kind of friend to have. Sticks with you, no matter what."

Corey's heart squeezed with jealousy. Then

she grew angry. If Ericka really liked that silly airhead, that was *her* problem.

"See you at the party," Ericka said. She made a sideways motion with her mouth. "You *are* still coming to the party, aren't you?"

"Of course." Corey tried to match the edge in Ericka's voice. "That is, *if* I'm still invited. Oh, and I might bring a date."

"Corey!" Ericka's cool front dissolved. "You're bringing a guy? Who is he? Do I know him?"

Corey gave a bright, hard smile. "Yeah, but I'd rather not say who he is. He might not come. He's not big on parties."

The warning bell rang.

Corey watched as Ericka, her eyes still wide and curious, hurried away to class. Let her wonder, she thought, heading for first period. It served her right. If Ericka could get Susan into the act, Corey felt under no obligation to tell her about Topher.

But would Topher even go to the party? She wouldn't hold her breath. She wasn't even sure she wanted to go. Especially now that Susan was involved.

Again the flare of jealousy. Corey quickened her steps to control the feeling. No, she wasn't really jealous. She just didn't want to go to Ericka's house where nothing had changed, knowing right up the road—

Don't. Don't think about it. She'd go to that party and try to have fun. Whether Topher went or not.

But when she saw Topher sitting behind his desk in algebra, she knew the party wouldn't be the same without him. Her heart gave a tug of joy when he flashed his crooked smile.

She sat down and watched shyly as Topher approached her. He dropped a folded slip of paper on her desk, then sauntered across the room to the pencil sharpener. Corey glanced around furtively, hoping Mr. Yenke hadn't seen. Then she opened the note. It was written in pencil, in dark angular strokes.

Corey: I'd like to talk to you after class. Wait for me?—Topher.

Corey read the note twice, then folded it again and slipped it into her pocket. She returned Topher's smile, and nodded. She could hardly keep her mind on Mr. Yenke's lesson.

CHAPTER
15

"THANKS FOR WAITING," Topher said when he met Corey in the hall a few minutes after class. "I had to talk to Yenke about something."

"Sure, it's okay." Corey tried to sound casual, but she could feel her heart beating against her ribs. She followed Topher to his locker, fumbling with the tie of her raincoat.

"Look," Topher said suddenly, "if your offer still stands, I think I'd like to go to that party."

"Great." Corey couldn't help but grin. Her first date! And with none other than Topher West.

"I guess I could wear my motocross stuff," Topher was saying. "Or go as a fire victim." A faint smile. "Tacky, huh? Well, what about you?"

"Oh, I don't know," Corey said. "Haven't really thought about it." She picked an empty milk carton off the floor and tossed it lightly on top of the pile of an overflowing trash can. "Maybe I'll go as a garbage can or something."

Topher laughed. "A garbage can—that's choice! The total opposite of you. You're always so neat. Not that that's bad. Well, I mean, you always look nice."

Corey felt her cheeks ignite. "Thanks," she mumbled. "Did you get any more land cleared on Sunday?"

"Yeah, that's why I was talking to Yenke. His sister works with my mom at the hospital and she told him about me. He's got a pickup truck. Offered to help me take a couple of loads of debris to the dump."

Corey's head jerked in surprise. "Mr. Yenke is *helping* you?" Her voice rose an octave. "But he's so mean. I can't imagine him helping anyone."

"People aren't just naturally mean," Topher said. "They always have a reason. Mom told me his wife died about ten years ago. Guess he never forgave her for that."

"I'm sorry about his wife," Corey said. "But he's still the worst teacher around, and I can't wait to get out of his class."

Topher took his books from his locker, shutting it with a determined bang. "I kind of like him," he said, half to himself. "We have a lot in common." He stood quietly for a moment, as if remembering something. "Well, gotta run. Too wet to work at the house today, but tomorrow, if it's clear, I'll give you a lift to the canyon to look for Jabberwocky."

"Thanks, but I'm supposed to meet with Anna Mendoza about her fire article. How about Wednesday?"

"Sure," Topher said. "See you."

On Tuesday, as promised, Anna let Corey proofread the fire article while they shared a large order of hot, crispy fries at McDonald's. By midweek the rain had let up. Corey spent both Wednesday and Thursday afternoons searching for Jabber in the canyon with Topher.

On Friday, in Yenke's class, Corey's gaze kept wandering to the thirty copies of the *Forge*, stacked neatly on the teacher's desk. She was anxious to see her interview in print.

She stole a glance at the clock and sighed. Then she noticed Mr. Yenke had turned away from the chalkboard. He stared pointedly at her.

"It is obvious," he said slowly, emphasizing every word, "that some of you are impatient to escape my class." Corey pretended to study her algebra book, her cheeks hot. Someone coughed nervously. "May I remind you that we still have five more minutes remaining in the period? When the bell rings, you may take this week's sophomoric trivia—" He waved his hand over the *Forge*. "—and then trot off to do whatever it is you do in your spare time. Until then, there is much we can accomplish in five minutes."

Sure, Corey thought, stifling a yawn. Like die of boredom.

When at last the bell rang, Mr. Yenke held up his hand for silence. "Your homework assignment on Monday—" He paused ominously. "—is pages two hundred and thirty-seven, thirty-eight, and thirty-nine."

Moans.

"But Mr. Yenke," someone complained, "it's Halloween!"

"I'm not aware that Halloween is a national holiday," the teacher replied dryly.

Boring, mean, *and* a slave driver, Corey thought. How could Topher like this man? They weren't even remotely alike.

Amidst more groans, she pushed her way to Mr. Yenke's desk and grabbed the first newspaper on the pile. She smiled, pleased to see her interview on the front page. She checked to make sure her ad for Jabberwocky had been printed as well. Yes, there it was. Anna had added Corey's new address, too.

Topher followed her outside. "I thought you might like to have an extra copy," he said.

Corey took the paper, smiling in thanks. Topher acted so nice these days. She had noticed he still presented a cold facade to people at school, but with her he was different. Warmer. Less distant. And he had dropped the biting insults that used to make her feel so foolish and angry. Granted, he hadn't opened up much since the day he cried, but he seemed perfectly willing to let Corey use him as her sounding board.

Corey had told him about her strange numb feeling and about her inability to cry. She also explained the bizarre changes in her parents and Pete. Topher didn't comment much, but he didn't criticize her either, and Corey had been grateful for the chance to talk. Topher was the only one who understood her need to return to the canyon.

"Do you want to go to the canyon again?" Topher was asking.

"No thanks. I'd better get home and do the homework Yenke the Slave Driver assigned. And get ready for Ericka's party."

"What time should I pick you up?"

"Oh, eight o'clock, I guess," Corey said. She noticed a tense expression on Topher's face. "What's the matter?"

"Nothing. It's just that—" Topher jerked his head. "I just feel strange about going to this party. I won't know anybody there, except you."

"That's okay," Corey said. "I feel strange about going too, and I'll know everybody." She stared at the pavement thoughtfully. "You know, it doesn't seem right going to a party when you have nothing to celebrate."

Topher nodded. "Yeah, well—see you tonight."

Corey waved and hurried to the parking lot to meet her mother. She skimmed Anna's article as she walked. The interview had been printed almost word for word. But wait a minute . . .

Corey slowed her pace. The ending had been rewritten since she read it on Tuesday. Originally, Anna had said something about the fire victims needing understanding and moral support. But now—

Because of the fire, Anna wrote, *Corey is facing a lot of changes in her life. Drastic changes. "I'm scared, " she told me. "I feel like everything and everyone I ever loved has been taken away. I feel empty. And very alone." But Corey has yet to realize she hasn't lost everything in this disaster. As long as she is alive, she will always have someone to help her face difficult changes and make new ones, better ones. That someone? Herself.*

Corey stared at the words until they blurred. What was Anna talking about? There was nothing she, Corey, could do to make things right again. Not without help from her parents, or Pete. And they had deserted her.

Corey ripped angrily at the thin paper of the *Forge* and flung the strips into a garbage can. Anna hadn't really understood after all. No one understood except Topher, and there was no way he could help her move back to the canyon, either.

Don't think about the before times, she thought during the ride home. Just—don't—think. It only made now worse. Corey resolved to concentrate on the party, forcing herself to feel excited about it, pretending to act thrilled when her mother questioned her about her costume.

But as eight o'clock approached, Corey discovered her anticipation was very real. Little bubbles of excitement burst inside her, sending a surreal tingle through her body. Did Topher know how to dance? Would he try to kiss her? What would they talk about?

"Your first date," Mrs. Johnson said dreamily, as if remembering her own. She frowned slightly at Corey's costume. "Are you sure you want to go dressed as a garbage can?"

Corey laughed, looking at herself in the mirror. She wore a green wool sweater, jeans, and a large plastic trash bag. Two holes had been cut in the bottom of the bag for her legs, two holes in the sides for her arms. The opening was tied at her shoulders Corey tilted a tiny plastic lid on her head, tying it under her chin with string. "Fire victims can't be choosers," she said cheerfully.

Her mother winced.

"Besides, Topher liked the idea. Honest, Mom."

"And the garbage?" Mrs. Johnson asked. "He wants you to wear that, too?"

"Oh, yeah. Almost forgot." Corey dumped the contents of her backpack on the floor. "I've been collecting empty wrappers and cartons from school all week. Just tape or staple them on the bag."

Mrs. Johnson rolled her eyes. Corey taped a few wrappers in her auburn hair, then smeared brown and green makeup on her face. At eight o'clock she stood ready.

Dr. Johnson peered up at her over an insurance pamphlet. He dropped the paper dramatically. "Well, you're not the same fairy princess I knew ten years ago, but—" He sniffed. "You do have a certain air about you. What's that cologne you're wearing? Eau de Trash?"

"Dad, you know I'm not wearing any cologne."

"Just the same, beware of stray dogs."

Corey was about to retort when lights flashed in the window. Her stomach flipped. A car had pulled into the driveway.

"Topher's here," she said. "He borrowed his mom's car for the evening."

"Good, I don't want you riding that motorcycle. Ever."

"Oh, Dad," Corey said, exasperated. She wanted to argue, but stopped herself. It was the only negative remark he'd made about her date with Topher. Even her mom had been strangely silent about it, saying only, "I'm glad you two have finally worked things out."

The doorbell rang.

Corey adjusted the popcorn bag on the front of her costume and opened the door. "Ta-daa!"

Topher laughed. "You look great."

"Thanks. Where's your costume?"

Topher shifted uncomfortably, a sheepish look on his face. "I don't have one. Couldn't think of anything."

"But you can't go without a costume," Mrs. Johnson said, stepping up behind Corey.

"Don't worry, Mom." Corey pulled Topher into the living room. "I won't let him get away with this. There's got to be something around here he can wear." Then she snapped her fingers. "I've got it! Dad, can Topher wear one of your white dentist jackets?"

"Sure, but—"

Topher interrupted. "Corey, I'm not sure that's a good idea." He glanced at Dr. Johnson as if remembering their first meeting. "I'm not the dentist type."

"No, not a dentist," Corey said. A sly smile. "A *mad* dentist. Like a mad scientist, you know?" She gave Topher a little push toward the bathroom. "Wait in there. I'll get the jacket, then Mom and I will see what else we can do to fix you up."

For the next twenty minutes, Topher stood helplessly while the two women fussed over him. Corey, wielding a curling iron and comb, ratted his blond, unruly curls until they stuck out at wild angles. Then she and her mother used eyebrow pencil to slant and darken his eyebrows. White eyeshadow was smeared last to make death circles under his eyes. As a finishing touch, they taped toothbrushes and strands of dental floss to the white jacket.

"Not bad," Corey mused. "But something is missing. Of course!" She ran to the kitchen, returning with a bottle of red food coloring. "Blood," she explained, dribbling the liquid down his front. She handed him a pair of rusty pliers. "Don't forget these for pulling teeth. Okay, you're ready. Let's go."

They started out the door.

"Wait a minute," Dr. Johnson called. "What's that on my good jacket? You're going to give us dentists a bad name."

"Oh, I don't know," Corey said. "I think Topher gives the profession character."

Her father shook his head. "Words like that from my own daughter. Out—out!" He laughed. "Have fun, kids."

"We will," Corey said. "I really think we will." She waved, then walked with Topher to the car.

CHAPTER
16

"Wow," TOPHER SAID when they arrived at Ericka's. "Your friend really knows how to throw a party."

Corey nodded. Jack-o'-lanterns, with comical and gruesome expressions, flickered in the semidark family room. A long table, pushed against one wall, was laden with Halloween cupcakes, candy, sodas, and popcorn. Couples danced to music blasting from the stereo.

"Those costumes—they're great," she said in amazement. There were witches and harem girls, cavemen and monsters; even an authentic-looking robot. "Topher, I feel like I'm wearing—garbage"

He laughed. "I wonder why. Want to dance? Or get something to eat first?"

"I'd better find Ericka and say hi. After all, this was supposed to be my party, too."

Topher followed her as Corey maneuvered to the kitchen, waving at kids she knew. She found one of Ericka's sisters making

140

more popcorn.

"Where's Ericka?" Corey shouted over the din of the music.

Outside, the girl pantomimed.

"Thanks!" Corey led Topher to a sliding-glass door. They stepped outside into the chilly night air.

"It's my first time I've been up here at night since—since the fire," Corey said. "It's so eerie." She shivered. Behind her, the house glowed warm with laughter and music, but Corey was aware only of the darkness stretching before her into desolation.

Her home. It used to be up there. But now it was a gaping hole. A toothless hole in a wide, laughing mouth. Like the pumpkins.

"Don't think about it," Topher said gruffly, but his hand on her arm was gentle.

"Corey!"

"There's Ericka," Corey said, grateful for the diversion.

"Hi, Corey. Glad you could make it." Ericka wore white tights and a hot-pink leotard that accented her tanned face and arms. Her blonde hair had been braided and pinned, Princess Leia style, under a gold crown. The oversized card she wore strapped over her shoulders bore a perfect reproduction of the Queen of Hearts. Susan Airhead stood beside her, dressed similarly as the King.

My costume idea, Corey thought in a flash of acid resentment. How could Ericka betray her like that? Her only consolation came when Ericka's eyes widened almost comically at the sight of Corey's date.

"You remember Topher?" Now Corey felt cool, in control.

"Oh, uh, sure. Glad you could come." Ericka smiled feebly through hot-pink lipstick. "Um, do you want to see our haunted house? Susan and I put it together."

One section of the patio was entirely enclosed by refrigerator boxes, cut open and lined up to form a twisting maze. Skeletons and arching black cats were painted in fluorescent colors along the walls. Corey watched as three girls, dressed as Mousketeers, hesitated at the entrance. A mummy's hand reached out to greet them. They screamed and giggled.

"Ladies first," Topher said.

"Oh, no—after you!"

"Okay, we'll go together." He took Corey's hand.

The pathway was dark and stuffy. Not frightening at all, Corey thought, though she jumped when a rubber spider dangling from a string brushed her forehead. She and Topher rounded a corner to find a dummy, drenched in ketchup, lying across their path. It grinned up at them ghoulishly, under black lights. There were similar scenes throughout the tunnel: plastic snakes, dime-store tarantulas, a severed doll arm hanging from the ceiling.

"Pretty corny, huh?" Topher whispered.

"Yeah. I hope we're near the end. It's hot in here." Corey stopped. "Hey, did you hear that?"

A low moan echoed through the maze.

Up ahead a girl said, "Hey, you guys. What was that noise?"

"Just the wind."

"Naw, I'll bet Ericka has one of those Halloween records playing. The ones with the dogs howling and stuff."

"That's no record. Listen!"

The chilling moan came again. It started low, then began to build, wavering on a sharp note.

"There it is again!"

"What is it?"

Susan gave a half-hearted laugh. "Funny, Ericka. Joke's over. Cut it out."

"I'm not doing it!" Corey heard her friend's voice behind them.

"Then what is it?"

"I don't know!"

Topher squeezed Corey's hand. It wasn't much warmer than her own.

Another moan. This time joined by several others. The strange cries rose into screams.

"Let's get out of here!" someone shouted.

Ericka squeezed past Corey in the narrow passageway. "Come on, this way." Topher obeyed immediately, pulling Corey with him.

"It's so dark," a girl whimpered. She sounded close to tears. "How do we get out?"

"Don't panic. Just follow me," Ericka urged. Too late. Several kids were already pushing

143

ahead, trying to find their own way out of the twisting maze. Corey felt an elbow in her ribs. A cardboard wall fell with a loud thud into the grass. Someone screamed.

"Where's it coming from?" Ericka asked. They were outside now, the low moans still filling the air.

"There," Topher said. He pointed to a large shrub at the edge of the Smiths' property. It had been burned to a half-skeleton in the fire.

Ericka snatched up a flashlight from the picnic table. The night seemed to swallow the beam. Then the light flashed on two red eyes and someone gasped. Corey felt a shiver trickle through her body. The moan broke off into a short cry, then the eyes disappeared into the brush.

Ericka switched off the flashlight, her giggle relaxing the group. "It's okay, guys. It's not the Great Pumpkin or the boogeyman. We just got trick-or-treated by a bunch of cats!"

A few kids laughed in relief.

"Um, Corey?" Topher began softly. "I really like holding your hand, but I think rigor mortis is setting in."

Corey released Topher's hand immediately, embarrassed. "I must've been scared," she said, stretching her fingers. "Sorry."

"Let's go inside."

Corey was following him to the house when suddenly Ericka's words clicked inside her mind.

144

"Wait a minute," she said, turning back to her friend. "Ericka, your dad's allergic to cats, isn't he? When did you get a cat?"

Ericka didn't look up. She was busy smoothing a crumpled corner of her card. "They're not really ours. I think they were orphaned by the fire," she said. "There's been about ten of them creeping around the house every night at dinnertime. We've tried to catch them, but they're really wild." She switched the flashlight on again, playing the beam along the bushes. "See? Already gone."

Corey felt a surge of anger. "Ericka," she began, barely able to control her voice. "Why didn't you tell me before about the cats? Jabberwocky could be one of them!"

"What are you talking about?" Ericka asked. She looked stunned. "Is Jabber missing?"

"Yes. He's been missing for two weeks. Since the fire. You know that."

"No. No, I didn't know." A pause. "How could I have known?" Ericka said, suddenly defensive. "You've been so tight-lipped since the fire. How was I supposed to find out, read your mind?"

"I told you," Corey said angrily. "You just forgot."

Ericka shook her head. "You didn't tell me."

Hadn't she? Corey thought, doubt tugging at her mind. Of course she had. She must have. She always told Ericka everything.

Ericka's tan seemed to have faded from her

face. She looked as pale as her blonde hair. "Why didn't you tell me about Jabber, Corey?" she asked. "As a matter of fact, why haven't you told me anything about the fire?"

"Never mind," Corey said. Her voice almost broke on the words. "You wouldn't understand."

Ericka started to say something. Then she noticed a group of kids standing nearby, listening. "Come on," she said. Quickly she led Corey into the house and down the hall to a small bathroom.

Corey sat on the counter, arms folded. "What are we doing in here? I've left Topher all alone."

"Just listen a minute," Ericka said, shutting the door. "I want to know why you think I wouldn't understand. I was here the night of the fire too, remember? I saw the flames. I watched our neighborhood burn down all around me. Do you know what it's like to live here now? Seeing everything destroyed? I'm reminded of it every day. How can you say I don't understand?"

"It's not the same thing," Corey said. "You're still here. That's the point. My house is gone. But yours didn't—" Corey stopped.

"So that's it," Ericka said. She looked directy into Corey's eyes. "Why don't you say it, Corey? But my house didn't burn, right?" Her voice grew louder. "It doesn't matter that I'm your best friend. My house didn't burn, so of course I couldn't possibly understand how you feel. Right, Corey? Right?"

Corey's lips quivered. She wanted to run away, but Ericka was blocking the door.

"That's why you've been avoiding me, isn't it?" Ericka demanded. "You're jealous. You can't accept the fact that your house burned and mine didn't. Well, what am I supposed to say? What can I do to make things right between us again? Tell you I wish my house *had* burned? Well, I can't say it, Corey. I'm sorry your house is gone. But I'm glad mine isn't. And no way will I feel guilty about it!"

Corey looked away. Her throat felt tight—her fists tighter.

"Corey," Ericka said. Her voice grew quieter, but it quivered a little. "I'm so sorry. I'm sorry I can't give you what you want. I can't feel guilty in order to keep our friendship." She paused, as if weighing her words carefully. "But when you stop resenting me, hating me—when you stop shutting me out, I'll be here. I'm still your friend, Corey. I always have been."

Corey's cheeks flamed with anger and bitterness. "Don't do me any favors," she said coldly. "I don't need friends like you."

Ericka looked as though she'd been slapped. She started to speak, but Corey pushed past her into the hall. In a moment, she was running through the house, running out to the driveway. She had to get away, get away fast. And she didn't care where.

CHAPTER
17

WHEN SHE REACHED the street, Corey stopped running. Her breath came in wild, sobbing gasps. Never had she felt so hurt, so angry. She needed to strike back—or explode.

With a sweeping motion, she scooped up a handful of rocks from the street. She hurled one against the side of the Smith's mailbox. It clanged loudly.

"It's not fair!" Corey cried. Another rock flew. "It's—" *Clang!* "—not—" *Clang!* "—fair!"

There were no rocks left. Corey looked down at her empty hand, willing more rocks to appear. It had felt so good to release some of her anger.

Footsteps. Corey turned to see Topher standing a few feet away, watching her solemnly.

"What are you looking at?" she demanded.

"You. Throwing a temper tantrum."

Corey wished she held another rock. She

would've thrown it at him with pleasure. "Leave me alone," she said.

"I can't. I have to take you home."

"I don't have a home, remember?"

"Come on," Topher said, gently taking her arm.

Touched by his tenderness, Corey obeyed. Her body felt suddenly limp, drained, but inside, her stomach still burned with anger. "Don't be so nice to me," she said crossly. "I don't know why, but—but it only makes things worse."

Topher dropped her arm.

"And you're not taking me home," she added.

"Okay. Fine. We'll go down to the beach. I want to talk to you."

Reluctantly, Corey followed Topher to the car. During the drive she noticed her trash-can hat was missing and her costume was torn. Oh, who cared? She rested her hot cheek against the cool windowpane, and stared out at the night.

When they reached the beach, Topher parked the car, the headlights flashing like ribbons of white steel on the dark sea. Corey crouched closer against the door, listening to the waves fold and break.

"Feel better?" Topher asked.

"No."

"If I talk, will you listen?"

Corey nodded. Topher was silent for so long that she wondered if he had even seen her head move. Then he spoke, his voice strained and quiet.

"I want to tell you something. I've never told anyone this before. Maybe it'll help you." He took a deep breath, then began speaking slowly. "Six years ago, when I was ten, my dad split. Just up and left home one night without telling anyone. Mom and I haven't heard from him since." At a small gasp from Corey, he said, "No, don't say anything. I'm not sorry he's gone. Things are better now than—before. He never was much of a father."

Corey ached inside for Topher. Although she and her dad were no longer close, at least she knew he was still there for her at times, like the night of the siren. But Topher's dad, he was really gone.

"Even though Dad was rotten," Topher continued, "I loved him. Funny, you know?" He shook his head. "But he was my father and it hurt, really hurt when he left. That's when I decided I was never going to love anyone else again. It hurt too much to love. So I started to shut people out of my life, hurting them before they could hurt me. I decided I didn't need anybody." A bitter laugh. "I don't know if I was punishing the world, or myself."

So that's why, Corey thought. Why he was always so aloof, so mean to everyone. Like Mr. Yenke. She remembered Topher's remark about him: *People aren't just naturally mean. They always have a reason.* Now she understood why Topher felt he and Mr. Yenke had something in common.

"I'm sorry," she whispered.

"I'm not telling you this so you'll feel sorry for me," Topher said angrily. "I've spent enough time feeling sorry for myself. And that was my mistake. I should've been more like Mom. She didn't pity herself at all. After Dad left, she went back to nursing school. Worked during the day and went to school at night. It took her years, but finally she got her degree and a good job at the hospital here. Corey, she worked so hard to buy that house for us in Sycamore Canyon. She wanted to give me a real home. And she knew she couldn't do it sitting around feeling sorry for herself. Like I was doing. Like you're doing."

"What are you talking about?" Corey said defensively.

"Stop ruffling your feathers and face it," Topher said. "You've got a terminal case of the 'Why me?' blues. I don't know if it's just the fire, or if what Ericka said is true about you being jealous—"

"How do you know what Ericka said?" Corey asked.

"She told me. Then sent me to look for you."

"Well, it's *not* true," Corey said.

"I didn't say it was. Will you just listen a minute?" Topher hit the steering wheel. The horn gave a short cry. "You said in Anna's interview that you feel alone. Well, it's your own fault. I've been listening to you talk all week, about your brother, your parents. I don't

151

think they've deserted you. You're the one who's shutting people out. People who care about you. Like Ericka."

"Ericka doesn't understand," Corey said.

Topher shook his head. "Maybe you've never given her a chance. She seems like a good friend."

"Well, you're wrong! What do you know about friendship, anyway? You've never had any friends." There. She had said something to hurt him. He deserved it.

Topher nodded. He didn't seem affected at all. "You're right. I alienated anyone who could've been my friend. Until two weeks ago, when I met you. Really met you for the first time."

A long silence. Corey listened to the waves crashing, waiting for him to go on.

"The night of the fire, you were amazing. Before, I thought you were just a dumb kid. But you showed me I was wrong. You didn't want that fire to burn your house, so you decided to fight it. I'll never forget the hard look on your face when you flew down the hill, ready to do anything to save your home."

Corey stared out the window, her eyes unblinking, stinging. She heard admiration in Topher's voice, but she didn't want to listen. Didn't want to remember. It hurt too much.

"That night, that week, changed something in me," Topher continued. "You changed something in me. I knew then that if I was tired of being alone and bitter and hurt I was going to have to get off my butt and do something about it—because no one else was going to do it for me." He sighed. "Corey, what I'm trying to say is, you've got to keep fighting, like the night of the fire. If you don't like your life, you've got to be the one to change it."

"I can't! I can't do it."

"Maybe you can't because you don't want to, Corey."

"No. That's not true! I can't do it. I don't know how. I want things to be the way they were before. I hate change. I hate it!"

She sat stunned at her own outburst. Her voice rang in her ears.

"I'd better take you back now," Topher said quietly. "It's getting late."

Corey didn't argue. She stared out the window, feeling drained and confused. The hard ice cube in her throat burned.

When they reached her house, Topher pulled on the emergency brake but left the engine running. "I used to feel the same way about change," he said. It was as if they hadn't stopped their conversation at the beach. "I hated change. I wish now I'd listened to Mom. She always says, 'Where there's a will, there's a way. Keep moving forward. Out of bad things can come good.'" He took Corey's hand. "Really corny, I know. That fire was bad. Almost as bad as my dad leaving. But Corey, if it hadn't been for the fire, I wouldn't have gotten to know you."

Corey swallowed hard, realizing suddenly that she felt the same way about him.

"You're special, Corey. Smart, funny, caring. And very brave. You're everything I ever wanted in a friend."

Corey shook her head. "I don't understand. If you're my friend, why are you saying things that hurt me? I thought you understood. You're just deserting me, too."

"No, I'm not," Topher said. "I'm behind you, all the way. But there comes a time when—when you can't depend on family or friends to make your life right. You have to do it yourself."

Corey jerked her hand away. "That's what all my so-called friends keep saying. Pete, Ericka. Even Anna in that stupid article. Well, I don't need any more 'friends' like you!"

Corey felt a stab of instant regret. She didn't mean it. She didn't mean it at all! It was just that she felt so confused, so alone. She had wanted to hurt Topher for hurting her . . .

She jumped suddenly when the engine gunned. Topher stared at her, his face the cold, blank mask of two weeks ago. He threw off the white dentist's jacket. It landed in her lap.

"Okay," he said. "Guess I was wrong about you. I should've know. Thanks for a lovely evening. You've proved I was right all along. Parties are a real drag."

He gestured for Corey to get out of the car. She stepped out onto the sidewalk. "Topher,

154

wait," she began. "I'm sorry, I didn't mean—"

Topher reached over, shutting the door in her face. Then he drove off, tires squealing. Corey stood alone and shivering in the night air, watching the red tail lights of Topher's car. The more they faded into darkness, the lonelier she began to feel.

. . . Everything and everyone I ever loved has been taken away . . .

Her own words pressed down upon her. Until that moment, she hadn't realized just how untrue they were. Sure, she had lost her home, her security. But Topher hadn't been taken away. *She had pushed him.*

Had she done the same with Ericka? Pete? Her parents? They'd all changed in little ways since the fire, but had they really stopped caring about her? Or had she just pushed them out of her life the way she had pushed Topher, the way Topher and Mr. Yenke had pushed away the world when their pain grew too sharp to bear?

I'm really alone now, Corey thought. "And it's all my fault," she said aloud. She closed her eyes, and her body swayed a little. "All my fault."

CHAPTER
18

THE NEXT AFTERNOON, Corey stood in front of the old mirror in her room, staring at her distorted reflection. "I'm sorry," she whispered to it, "I've been acting like a jerk and—" She stopped. What was the point in practicing things she'd never have the courage to say? She couldn't face Ericka again. And as for Topher . . .

Topher.

Corey sat down on the sleeping bag, hugging her knees against her chest. Nothing she could say would make things right between her and Topher again. No apology could erase the hurt she had caused him. After years of hiding inside himself, he had finally opened up to one person: her. He had stretched out his hand, wanting her friendship, and what had she done? Thrown that friendship in his face. Now he would close up again like a clam, submerging deeper than ever before so no one could reach him again. Especially her.

How she wished she had the nerve to call him! She longed to tell him how sorry she was. More important, she wanted to thank him. After all, he hadn't meant to hurt her. He had only tried to save her from the years of pain he'd gone through by shutting people out.

"Corey," her mother called through the door. "Are you finished with your homework yet?"

"Almost," Corey said. She sighed, glancing at the unopened algebra book. She had lied to her parents, pretending to be swamped with schoolwork so they wouldn't disturb her. She'd spent all day in her room, thinking about the night before.

"Honey, do you mind if I talk to you for a minute?" Mrs. Johnson asked.

"I—I guess not."

Corey looked up as her mother came in and sat down on a rickety chair. She noticed there were dark smudges under her mother's eyes. Corey glanced quickly away.

"I came to apologize," Mrs. Johnson said. "I had other things on my mind at breakfast this morning, and I didn't even ask you how the party was."

Corey had a sudden desire to throw herself into her mother's arms, crying, *It was awful, Mom! I had a fight with Ericka, and Topher'll probably never speak to me again, and—* But she only shrugged. "It was okay, I guess."

"I give you so much credit, Corey," her

mother said. Her voice was almost a whisper. "I don't think I would've been brave enough to go to that party."

"What do you mean?"

"It's a terrible thing to say, but—I'm so jealous, so resentful of the Smiths. I'd give anything to have it be their house that burned, and not ours!"

Corey's head jerked up. Her mother did understand. She did!

"I'm so proud of you for going," Mrs. Johnson continued. "Funny to think that my baby daughter is stronger than her old mom."

"But I'm *not*—" Corey began.

"You went to that party," her mother said. "And you've been to the canyon, seen the ruins. No, don't deny it. Mrs. Robles mentioned she saw you and Topher there the other day. I'm not mad, honey. I think it's great the way you can face this thing head-on, where I . . . ? All I want to do is run and hide, forever."

But you can't, Mom, Corey thought. Otherwise you'll end up old and mean and unhappy, like Mr. Yenke. Or alone and lonely, like me . . .

Her mother stood up. She wiped quickly at the tears in her eyes, then forced a smile. "Didn't mean to come in and start a flood. Actually, Dad and I are going out for a ride. We thought maybe you'd like to come along. You've been studying all day. Don't you think you could use a break?"

"Probably. But I want to be alone for—for

a little longer. But thanks anyway, Mom."

Her mother started for the door. "Corey, I know you're unhappy here. I just wish—well, I want you to know that Dad and I, we're always ready to listen. Really."

Corey nodded. Then she stood up and gave her mother a quick hug. Mrs. Johnson hugged back, her arms warm and comforting. She looked at Corey as if waiting for her to say something, but Corey broke away. Mrs. Johnson shut the door softly behind her.

Corey listened to her mother's steps recede down the hall. She wanted to call after her, feel her mother's arms around her again, but then what? What could she say? Corey was so confused. She felt as if she'd pushed her parents so far that there was no way to get them back. Sure, she understood their pain a little better now. But how could she face it, deal with it, when she hadn't even dealt with her own pain?

The phone rang. Then twice more.

"Mom?" No answer. "Dad?" Her parents must've left. Wearily, Corey went into the kitchen and picked up the receiver.

"Corey? It's Ericka. Please don't hang up."

"I wasn't going to," Corey said quickly. A pause. She could hear her own heart beating nervously in her ears.

"Look, Corey," Ericka was saying. "I know you don't consider me your friend anymore, but I wanted to tell you something as—as an old friend." She spoke hurriedly, uneasily, as if she had to say the words fast or not at all. "There's a cat that's been hanging around here that sort of looks like Jabber. I didn't realize it before because—well, I honestly didn't know Jab was missing."

Jabberwocky! Corey felt a jolt of hope.

"I thought you might like to come up and have a look," Ericka continued. "The cats usually show up at dark, around five. Come early and wait. Otherwise you'll spook them."

Corey found speaking difficult. "Thanks. Thanks so much, Ericka."

"Sure. Don't bother to ring the bell. Just go around to the backyard. My family won't mind, and I'll stay inside. That way you won't have to see me."

"Oh, Ericka, you don't have to—"

"I hope it's him, Corey." Ericka hung up.

Corey replaced the receiver slowly, and then, in a panic, whirled to look at the clock. Four-thirty. No time to ride the bike. It'd be dark soon. And who knew when her parents would get back? Corey's stomach twisted in frustration. Rats! Her one real chance to find Jabberwocky, and she had no way to get to Ericka's.

Except—Topher.

Quickly, she flipped through the phone book looking for the number of his motel, cursing softly when the thin pages kept sticking together. There it was.

She dialed.

"Room one-oh-eight, please."

Oh, let him be there. Please, let him talk to me.

Come on, somebody answer the phone . . .

"Topher!" she cried when she heard his voice.

An ominous pause.

Corey sobered immediately. "I—I know you don't want to talk to me, Topher. But please, I need your help."

"What's wrong?" He seemed to sense the urgency in her voice. "Has something happened?"

"It's Jabberwocky. Ericka just called. She thinks he's one of those cats that've been hanging around her house. Topher, it's got to be him. I need to get up there before dark. Can you—"

"I'll be there in ten minutes."

Relief swelled inside her. Topher was going to help.

Maybe he hadn't closed her off after all.

Hastily, Corey wrote a note for her parents. Then she grabbed her jacket and ran outside to wait. When Topher pulled up a few minutes later, he said only, "Hold on tight."

"It's okay," she said. "I'm not afraid of the cycle anymore." She wrapped her arms around his waist.

Thank you. Thank you for coming, she thought, and held him tightly because he was her friend.

The evening had grown dusky when they reached the canyon. Corey led the way through the side gate to the back of Ericka's house. She and Topher crouched in the quiet shadows and waited.

Night draped over them like a hood. In the distance, television voices laughed, emphasizing the loud, deepening silence of the canyon. Corey became aware of Topher's even breathing beside her. Then there was a soft rustling in the brush.

"The wind?" Topher whispered.

Corey shook her head. The night felt cold, but there was no breeze. Her body tingled in anticipation.

In the next instant, she jumped, hearing a step behind her. The rustling noise stopped. Corey turned. "Ericka," she said.

"Sorry," her friend whispered. "I couldn't wait inside. I wanted to see if it was Jabber."

"Shhh." Topher put a finger to his lips. "Look." The two girls followed his gaze. An early moon was rising. It threw a cool, ethereal light across the yard. More rustling sounds. Then one by one, the cats slowly appeared. They moved forward, then froze. Forward. And stopped. Corey held her breath, watching. She forgot that Topher and Ericka knelt beside her in the cool grass. There were only the cats, appearing like stars from behind a cloud. Their eyes blinked bright and cold like stars, too.

A breath escaped Corey's lips.

The cats began moving again, braver now despite the moonlight.

"Mom left food for them in the grass," Ericka whispered. "There's the one I thought was Jabber. Over there. The black one."

Corey strained to see. The moon was higher now, but the cats were still half hidden in shadow. Was it Jabber? Only one way to find out.

Topher grabbed her hand. "Where are you going?"

"I've got to get closer. I can't see from here."

"Go slow," Ericka whispered. "They're so wild, you'll scare them."

Corey nodded. She crossed the yard, choosing her steps carefully, quietly.

A twig snapped.

Corey froze, afraid the cats would dart away. They seemed not to notice her, still gulping at their food.

Corey moved again. As she grew closer, she could see about a dozen cats. Their fur was matted and dirty and most of them were thin.

She knelt in the dirt. She was now only four feet away. "Jabberwocky," she called softly. "Here, Jabber." She held out her hand as if offering food.

The black cat looked up at her with fearful but hungry eyes.

Was it Jabber? Was it?

The cat approached hesitantly. The moon rose higher, flooding the backyard. Corey could see perfectly now. She made a low, strangled sound. The cat sniffed her hand and she smoothed his dusty fur, even though she knew for sure that it wasn't Jabberwocky.

The cat sniffed her hand again, then darted

back to the food dish.

Corey straightened slowly. She stood, arms limps at her sides, watching the cats for a long moment.

"It's not him," she said, her voice empty. Jabberwocky, she realized, was gone forever.

CHAPTER
19

"IT'S NOT HIM," Corey repeated dully as she rejoined her friends.

She walked past them to the patio and sat down on a wicker couch, hugging her knees. Ericka sat beside her. Topher lay down on a lounge, still gazing out at the backyard and the canyon beyond.

"I'm sorry, Corey," Ericka said. She sighed. "I really loved that little guy."

Corey nodded mutely. She didn't know what to say, what to feel. She had hoped for so long, and now that hope was gone.

"He was such a nutty cat," Ericka was saying. She smiled. "I'll never forget the day I came over to your house and he was asleep on the railing of your deck. We must've been about eight. Remember how he used to get excited and roll over when you called his name?"

Corey smiled too, remembering. "Yeah."

"I came over to play," Ericka continued,

"and there was Jab, sleeping on the railing. So I said, 'Hi, Jabberwocky!' He quivered, sort of like he was smiling, and then he rolled over. Right off the balcony. Must've fallen fifteen feet."

Topher turned to look at the girls. Ericka laughed at his expression.

"Corey's face looked exactly like yours, Topher. She screamed and ran to the railing. And there was Jab, slinking his way back up the hill. Not a scratch on him. But he looked so embarrassed!"

Corey giggled, caught up in the story. "You should've seen him, Topher. Covered with burrs and weeds. He just glared at Ericka, his whiskers twitching, like it was all her fault. If looks could kill, she would've been cremated."

The image seemed to form slowly in Topher's mind. Suddenly, he threw back his head and laughed. Caught up in the sound, Corey and Ericka laughed, too. They fell against each other, holding their stomachs, laughing until they couldn't breathe.

"We—shouldn't—be—laughing," Ericka gasped between giggles. "Poor—poor Jabber!"

"I know," Corey said, trying to pull a stern face. But with one glance at each other, both girls burst into another fit of laughter.

It felt so good to laugh with Ericka, Corey thought. So good to feel comfortable around her again. And what better person to laugh with than someone who had known Jabber, had loved him?

And more important, with someone who loved *her*.

Oh, Jabber. Funny Jabber. Gone.

Tears spilled down Corey's cheeks. She choked on a sob. Then she felt a rush, as if the ice cube inside were finally melting. She began to cry. For Jabber. For her home. For all the awful things she had said and felt and done in the last two weeks.

Ericka put an arm around her. "It's okay," she said.

Corey nodded, gulping for air, tasting her salty tears.

After a while, she dried her face on her jacket sleeve.

"I'm sorry," she said hoarsely. "Both of you. I'm sorry for everything."

Ericka was wiping away her own tears. "It's okay," she repeated.

"No, it isn't," Corey insisted. She hesitated for a moment, feeling tense and awkward, then forced herself to say the words. "You were right, Ericka. I've been so jealous of you, because your house didn't burn. I wanted my life to be normal again, like yours. I never thought that the fire had affected you, too. If I'd given you a chance to talk, to listen, maybe—maybe I would've found that out sooner."

Ericka gave a little sigh of relief. "I've missed you, Corey. Missed talking to you, being with you. That's why I went ahead with the party. I thought it might bring us back together. It really hurt when you ignored me. I thought you hated me."

"I guess I did, for a while," Corey answered. "But not anymore." She leaned over and hugged her friend. "I'm really sorry, Ericka."

Ericka hugged her back. "I'm sorry, too."

"Hey, I'm sorrier."

"No, *I* am!" The tense moment had passed. They were joking now, smiling again.

Corey turned to look at Topher. She felt more confident now. "Topher, you were right, too," she began softly. "I've been feeling really sorry for myself. See, my parents and Pete have always sort of protected me, always helped me with my problems. But after the fire, they had their own problems to worry about. I couldn't come first with them anymore, and that scared me. So I accused them of not caring about me. Not understanding. But how could they, when I never even tried to explain? I expected them to *know*. I expected them to think and feel the same way I did. I expected them to take away all my unhappiness . . ."

Her voice trailed off. She sat staring past Topher, as if seeing something clear for the first time. "But they can't," she whispered. "They can only do so much. I have to do the rest."

"An independent cat . . . ," Topher murmured.

Corey's eyes focused on him again. "Yes," she said, after a moment. "Yes."

"Well, you can count on our help."

"Really?" Corey almost whispered the word. Topher gave her his crooked smile. "Really."

Corey felt that familiar *zing* of anticipation, just as she always did during the Santa Anas. Topher hadn't crawled back into his shell. He was still there, still reachable. And if he was, maybe her parents and Pete were, too.

Corey stood up and wandered back out into the yard, gazing down into the moonlit canyon. Part of her felt sad. A piece of her life was gone forever. And yet, by crying and talking with her friends, some of the pain that had weighted her down was released, replaced by quiet acceptance—and a new spark of determination. Corey felt lighter, almost as if she could float.

"It's beautiful," she said.

Ericka followed her to the yard. She gave her friend an odd look. "But—it's *burned.*"

Corey nodded. "I know. But look at the grass. Even with just that bit of rain we had, it's starting to grow again." She stared in amazement at the tiny shoots, peeking up through the ash and dirt. They shone green-silver in the moonlight. "Just think, in the spring everything will be green again. You know, I've wished so hard that life could be the way it was before. I never realized things could change and still be beautiful." She sighed. "I wish Mom and Dad could see this. Maybe then they'd understand, too."

"I wish you could move back to the canyon," Ericka said.

"So do I," Corey said wistfully.

Topher came up behind her. She turned, and his gaze held hers for a long moment. The intense, blue eyes that Corey had once thought so ice-cold and distant, were now like a hand that was slowly uncurling, opening, revealing and offering an option. His eyes seemed to say: *You want to go home? Then* do *it.*

Corey suddenly recalled his words of the night before. *There comes a time when you can't depend on family or friends to make your life right. You have to do it yourself.*

Corey took a sudden deep breath. "Okay," she said slowly. "I'll do it." She spoke directly to Topher, as if taking that opening hand into hers. "I'll talk to my parents tonight. Really talk to them this time. As an adult, not a baby. And I'll listen, too. Try to understand their feelings, their reluctance. I know there aren't any guarantees. I might never move back to the canyon. Maybe Mom and Dad really are happy in the new house. But maybe, just maybe they just need more time than I did to realize that—that you can't run away from change."

Topher grinned at her. Corey grinned back, feeling as if his smile had touched her gently, warmly, for just a moment, on her cheek.

EPILOGUE

S PRINGTIME.

Corey sniffed the fresh, scented air. Once, not too long ago, summer had been her favorite time of year. Not after today. Now April and spring would forever smell warm and special in her mind.

I'll probably grow up with a wet cement fetish, too, Corey mused. She watched as the thick stuff slowly flowed out of the cement mixer. The dank, gritty smell filled her nostrils. She smiled. Today, the foundation was being poured for the Johnsons' new home in Sycamore Canyon.

"Hey, Sis!"

Corey turned to see Pete's new Honda pull up the driveway. She waved to her brother and Topher, then laughed when she saw Ericka and Anna crawling out of the cramped back seat, loaded with a picnic basket, sodas, and a camera.

"Thanks for inviting me," Anna said, slinging the camera on its strap over one shoulder. "This is the kind of news that makes a great front-page headline: *Fire Victims Rebuild Their Spirit As They Rebuild Their Homes.* Nice ring to it, huh?"

Corey grinned. "Sure. Why don't we walk up there a ways? You'll have a good view for your pictures."

The five of them climbed the hill above the Johnson property, sitting in the soft new grass.

Ericka spritzed open a Coke and took a sip. "Got to hand it to you, Corey. I never thought you'd talk your parents into rebuilding."

"Nothing to it," Corey replied airily. "Just a few patient, rational conversations."

Topher grunted. "Huh. It was my back-breaking labor that finally convinced them, and you know it."

Corey laughed. The previous November, Topher, Ericka, and Anna had worked long hours, helping her after school. They cleared most of the rubble from her property—with the help of Mr. Yenke's truck—then planted and watered grass seed. By mid-December, their work was finished. Corey then coaxed her family up to the canyon, promising a surprise.

"You four did all this work yourselves?" Dr. Johnson had said. He looked at Corey with pride, as if suddenly seeing her as the adult she was becoming.

"But why, Corey?" Mrs. Johnson asked,

putting her arms around her daughter. "Why did you do all this work, knowing Dad and I might not want to move back here?"

"Well," Corey began, "remember how you used to give me a hard time about teasing Pete about his car?"

Her mother nodded.

"You said once that someday there'd be something that *I* wanted bad enough to work for. That then I'd understand how much that car meant to Pete. Well, I wanted to show you and Dad that I *do* understand. That I'm willing to work to get us back to the canyon . . ." Corey's voice trailed softly. "And Mom, if you and Dad decide that the canyon isn't the place you want to be, well—I'll understand that, too. At least I'll know that I gave it my best shot."

Mrs. Johnson hugged her daughter again. "You did a wonderful job, Corey," she said through tears. "And you know? It's actually beautiful up here. I never thought anything would grow back. I guess there are some things that never change."

True, Corey thought, looking back on that day. The sun rose every morning. A rock, if dropped from her hand, would fall to the ground. But how you dealt with those facts— and the things that *did* change—that made all the difference in how you lived.

Maybe life was sort of like a river. Some people, like Pete and Ericka, flowed more easily with the changing currents. Sure, at times they got hung up on the rocks, stuck in eddies or pools where they didn't want to be. But they were willing to try another route, willing to find a way to paddle out into the mainstream again.

Then there were people like her parents, and Topher. They had tested the water, but when they felt the strong currents, for a time they were afraid to even get their feet wet.

And me? Corey shook her head, remembering. She had dug her feet in the mud, trying not to grow up, trying to escape, until she had washed over the falls. But not anymore.

Corey smiled down at the cement foundation, imagining the new house that would grow there in the months to come. It would not be as big or as beautiful as the old home, the one filled with special memories of Jabberwocky and motorcycles and childhood. But this new house would be special in a way the old one could never be, because she had gained the confidence and independence to help build it.

She closed her eyes, letting the warm breeze flirt with her hair. "I love it here," she said, to no one in particular.

"It sure isn't the boring neighborhood Mom and I first moved into eight months ago," Topher teased. "Listen to that ruckus!"

Throughout the canyon echoed hammers and saws. Men shouted and trucks labored and groaned under heavy loads. Every week, more and more people began to rebuild. New homes were springing up as fast as wildflowers after a rain.

Corey smiled, listening.

Topher took her hand in his. "What's so funny?" he asked.

"Nothing." She squeezed his hand.

Corey was listening to the sound of change—and she liked it.

ABOUT THE AUTHOR

LEE WARDLAW says, *"Corey's Fire* is based on a true story. Several years ago, a brush fire in Santa Barbara destroyed my family's home. I lost everything—including my cat. Days later, while sifting through the wreckage and ash, I found only two recognizable items: my old baby spoon and our front door knob! I kept both as souvenirs of what I call the 'before time.'

"In the aftermath of the fire, I met and talked with dozens of young people whose homes were also lost. I was impressed by their heroic attitude, the 'fire' they felt inside to rebuild their lives. And so I wrote *Corey's Fire* in their honor—and in honor of my family."

A former elementary school teacher, Lee is the author of more than a dozen books for young readers, including *Seventh-Grade Weirdo* and *Don't Look Back*. She lives in the Santa Barbara (California) foothills with her husband and two cats.